The Rose Bush

Carmen Bouldin

The Rose Bush

For Edgar A. Poe, with love.

Table of Contents

Annabel Lee

It was many and many a year ago,
In a kingdom by the sea,
That a maiden there lived whom you may know
By the name of Annabel Lee; —
And this maiden she lived with no other thought
Than to love and be loved by me.

I was a child and *she* was a child,
In this kingdom by the sea;
But we loved with a love that was more than love —
I and my Annabel Lee —
With a love that the wingéd seraphs in Heaven
Coveted her and me.

And this was the reason that, long ago,
In this kingdom by the sea,
A wind blew out of a cloud, chilling
My beautiful Annabel Lee;
So that her high-born kinsmen came
And bore her away from me,
To shut her up in a sepulchre,
In this kingdom by the sea.

The angels, not half so happy in Heaven,
Went envying her and me —
Yes! — that was the reason (as all men know,
In this kingdom by the sea)
That the wind came out of the cloud by night,
Chilling and killing my Annabel Lee.

But our love it was stronger by far than the love
Of those who were older than we —
Of many far wiser than we —

And neither the angels in Heaven above,
Nor the demons down under the sea,
Can ever dissever my soul from the soul
Of the beautiful Annabel Lee: —

For the moon never beams, without bringing me dreams
Of the beautiful Annabel Lee;
And the stars never rise, but I feel the bright eyes
Of the beautiful Annabel Lee: —
And so, all the night-tide, I lie down by the side
Of my darling — my darling — my life and my bride,
In her sepulchre there by the sea —
In her tomb by the sounding sea.

by Edgar Allan Poe

Chapter 1

Breakfast has always been my favorite meal of the day, thinking to myself as I waited for my parents to arrive in the dining room. Looking out the window was quite picturesque as I could watch the morning high tide roll out to begin each day anew. I had decided to take my drawing tablet to the beach since the weather would be quite lovely today.

"Good morning, Annabel. You are up bright and chipper this morning." My mother greeted me with a grin. As I daydreamed about the sea, I finally heard her. "Annabel, are you in a trance, dear?" She said as she snapped her fingers at me.

"Oh, I am sorry Mother. I was just excited because I am going out to the beach to sketch." I answered smiling from ear to ear.

"Sweet child, that sounds wonderful, but do take a blanket, a scarf, and a hat. You do not want to catch cold. Your father and I will be in the garden most of the day. There is fungus growing on one of the rose bushes we need to treat along with some weeding. I do wish you would join us some days." Mrs. Allan suggested.

"Mother, I love drawing. How about next weekend I join you in the garden and sketch some of your beautiful rose bushes, plants, or other flowers?"

"Annabel, I would love nothing better. Your father would also love the idea."

"What idea would I love?" Mr. Allan asked as he finally joined them for breakfast.

"Dearest, next weekend, Annabel is going to do some drawings in the garden." Mrs. Allan responded.

"Yes Father, I had not thought of the idea before now. Today, I am going to the beach. I love the *sounding sea*. It truly gives me so much inspiration." Annabel added dreamily.

Her father added, "That sounds delightful. I would love to see your art hanging in our home. You not only have a passion for what you do, but you are quite talented. Please do not ever give up your art." He paused to eat a bite of his eggs before he began again, "Wait, Adalaide, next weekend is our trip to Richmond. You are to accompany me. Annabel, we will not be here, so you will be staying with Aunt Sarah. So, plan two weekends from now to do your sketches in the garden."

I said with glee, "Yes Father. I love staying with Aunt Sarah. I am also excited about sketching the garden for you. I must do that after you return from your trip when we come back home together. This is so exciting! I love you both so much!"

Chapter 2

The following weekend arrived quickly. Aunt Sarah lived in town, so the carriage ride on Friday afternoon moved quickly. My parents dropped me off on the way to the train station. We said our goodbyes before I walked into her home. "Mother and Father, I am going to miss you."

"We will miss you too, Annabel. Please be on your best behavior for Aunt Sarah. I love you child." Mrs. Allan said with slightly tearful eyes.

Mr. Allan added, "Daughter, I know you will be the epitome of good manners for your Aunt. Keep practicing on your art. We want to see you grow up and add paintings in museums one day. We will only be gone a few days."

"Thank you, Father. I love you both. I do not know what I would do without you and the encouragement you give me. I am so humble for your praise." I whispered tearfully.

"Sweet Annabel, do not worry. We will be back before you can blink. Just remember, do not ever lose your passion for art. Your mother and I will always support you in any venture to accommodate your needs for your talent. We are staying at the Hotel Southerby, and your aunt knows this. She will take great care of you. We love you. See you in a few tomorrows." My father explained as he and my mother stepped back into the carriage. I watched as they rode away on the dusty street before entering my aunt's home.

Chapter 3

Aunt Sarah was the best aunt in the world—she was my only aunt—come to think of it, so that automatically made her the most delightful relative. However, I loved her almost like I loved my own mother, they were sisters after all. Yet, Aunt Sarah was a trifle different than my mother. My mother always planned everything just so where every party, every dinner, every everything was just as perfect as she wanted it to be. On the other hand, Aunt Sarah did make plans every now and then, but on a whim and a prayer. Once, I stayed with her for a whole week and what she said we would do when I arrived was the actual opposite of what was accomplished. She had planned on us having two dinner parties and attending another with one of her friends. We ended up going to the one dinner party and then traveling to Boston to shop for three days.

Being around both Mother and Aunt Sarah have provided me with the best of both worlds to grow up in. At only fifteen years old, I felt as if I could choose to someday grow up to have a little bit of both personalities stewing in my brain. Aunt Sarah never married that I am aware, but she is no old maid. She does what she wants within the delicate social graces approved of for a lady in society living alone. At just this moment, I realized I never asked her why she was not married, but maybe it was a subject too outrageous to suggest in conversation. I will ponder that for later.

I unpacked a few items I brought for the weekend, my parents would return on Monday to pick me up as we would travel home. I brought a simple dress in case we stayed around her house where I could go outside and sketch in her back yard. I also brought my best dress in case we were to have a dinner party or attend one. Even at my age, I learned from Aunt Sarah early on, I must be prepared for any situation. After situating my things, I walked into the parlor to ask my aunt what she had planned for us. "Aunt Sarah, I have unpacked, and I am ready for whatever adventure you are ready to endeavor."

"Well, tonight we will have a simple evening. My cook is preparing ham for supper. I asked her to make those little cakes you like for dessert. How does that sound? After we eat, I had planned to work on some of my embroidery. Dear, did you bring your sketching tablet? You may draw while I embroider, and you can fill me in on everything that has been going on in your end of town by the sea." Aunt Sarah suggested.

"That sounds wonderful. I can practice drawing your cat. Where is Catty?" I asked.

"She's milling about somewhere. During the day, you know she loves to sleep in the window seat, but I have not seen her perching there today. Check upstairs in my room. She may be hiding, silly old girl."

"Yes Auntie." I replied as I quietly started up the mahogany stairs to the second floor. I began looking under furniture for Catty, but I could not find her. I finally looked under

Aunt Sarah's bed, and I still did not see her. However, I did find a little flat case. I looked it over and was not sure what it was. Upon inspection, it seemed to have a little clasp on one end centered just so. I fiddled with it, and to my surprise, it opened. It contained a picture on one side. It was not a small portrait, but an actual picture. I read something about these in the newspaper. If memory serves me, I think it is called a dag-ger-o-something…um, a daguerreotype! That's it! What is Auntie doing with something like this? Especially since it was a picture of a man I had never seen before. Had it dropped onto the floor by accident? Or did she put it under the bed? I mustn't ponder about this; moreover, I might anger her if she knew I found it. I'll place it back where I found it for now. If the moment is right, maybe I can ask her later. Back to searching for Catty.

My aunt had several pillows on the bed and so I started moving them. As I continued this task, the covers started squirming as if a snake was rousing up underneath. The next thing I knew, there was Catty creeping cautiously out from the coverlet on my aunt's bed. Catty stretched in the fashion I like to call scaredy cat because her back arches up high and her tail shoots straight up into the air. Catty was a sleek calico marked as if the mixture of colors in her fur were quilted in oblong patterns around her back. She was gorgeous at even the ripe old age of thirteen. She still loved to play, loved to hunt, and loved to cuddle. My aunt was my favorite person, but Catty was my favorite animal—a bonus when I came to visit. I led my favorite feline down the stairs so I could feed her before we ate, then I knew she would be ready after supper to sit tidy on my aunt's ottoman where I could practice my skills on cat drawing.

We had supper at six and I thanked the cook, Mrs. Prosper, for my favorite cakes. She was giddy as a school girl as she pleased me so. Auntie and I moved into the parlor as Catty followed us and sat in her predictable spot upon the ottoman. She always stayed close to my aunt. "Catty is such a precious kitty. I love visiting her, too."

"She is that! Annabel, tomorrow I thought we would go shopping after dinner, so if you want to do some sketching outside, I would plan on rising early."

"Yes, ma'am." I answered, but still thinking about the daguerreotype hiding under her bed. Tonight was just not the time to ask her. Maybe tomorrow.

Chapter 4

Morning rituals began as repetitious as a church bell rattling its music on a Sunday morning; however, it was Saturday in my aunt's home. I was anxiously ready to go shopping in town. After breakfast, I ran up the stairs to retrieve my sketchbook so I could enjoy the morning in my aunt's garden. Upon leaving my room with my drawing accoutrements, I heard a noise in Auntie's room, so I peeked in and called her name, but there was no answer. Out of the corner of my eye, I saw the case holding the daguerreotype was now placed upon her dresser, and it was open. She must have realized it fell under the bed.

"Annabel, are you looking for me?" She asked as she came up behind me.

"No Aunt Sarah, I thought I heard a noise in your room, and so I looked in to see what it was."

"Well, I see you have your drawing tools. Are you heading outside?"

"Yes, ma'am." I felt a little uneasy thinking she might have the idea I was being nosy, so I tried to answer shortly.

"Wonderful, you have about two hours, then we will have dinner, and then walk to the shops. Do enjoy yourself out in the backyard." She sweetly replied.

I tried walking away, not looking too suspiciously. It seemed she had no clue I was being a little spy about her secret daguerreotype. That settles it, while we walk to the shops, I will ask her."

The morning in the backyard proved to be an excellent time for drawing. I practiced my landscaping skills in Auntie's lovely garden. Her garden was not as large as my parents' garden, and lacked the modicum of flowers and plants they so delicately managed, but her garden was simple and elegant—an inviting little paradise behind a house in town. As I drew, I realized this was perfect practice for preparing to draw my parents' garden. Starting with something basic would allow me to do a better job with all the intricate details of the floral varieties they possessed. I was so engrossed with my work, I barely heard Mrs. Prosper call me into supper. "Annabel, supper is ready."

"On my way, Mrs. Prosper!"

Supper proved to be quite delicious with a spread of meats, cheeses, breads, sauces, and jellies. "Annabel, I will just be a moment to get ready to walk to the shops. Why don't you get your things and meet me outside in about ten minutes?"

"Auntie, I will be waiting." I excitedly agreed as I went to get my little reticule and hat.

As I waited outside, the daguerreotype haunted my mind as a ghost lingering in a doorway. I must gain the courage to ask her. All she could do was tell me to mind my own business.

"Annabel, are you ready?" Aunt Sarah asked as she came down the stairs in a different dress, one appropriate for a day in town.

"Ready as I will ever be."

The shops were only about fifteen minutes from my aunt's house, but sometimes she liked to stroll more slowly because she enjoyed admiring her neighbor's flowers and plants. "Ooh, Mrs. McNamara's forsythia bushes bloomed so vibrant this year. I think their yellow looks just like a canary."

"Auntie, you may now call her yard the one with the canary bushes." I laughed, and she laughed, so I felt this was just the right time to ask her about the obsession I had developed. "Aunt Sarah, when I was looking for Catty yesterday, I perused many places in your bedroom, including under your bed before I found her. I must confess, I found the little case and opened it. I saw the daguerreotype, but I quickly closed it and placed it right back where I found it. I felt guilty for prying into your things. I humbly apologize."

"Annabel, I accept your apology, and it is okay. When I was your age, I was just as inquisitive as you. I guess we are a set of curious cats." She laughed before going on, "I guess now, as I am looking at your face, you want to ask me about the gentleman in the daguerreotype." Watching me with eyes glued to mine.

"Uh, yes, that thought did cross my mind." Responding hesitantly.

"First, before I tell you, how did you know what a daguerreotype was? They have only been taken for around three years. I think the first one was done in 1839." Auntie quizzed.

"I read the newspaper every day and there was an article about them about two years ago. I found them fascinating."

"I see, I always forget how truly intelligent and talented you are for such a young lady." She added, "Well, the gentleman you saw was a man who had courted me since 1838. I know I was considered an old maid by the time we began our courtship, but I knew him when we were young. Our families used to live next door to each other, and we were grand friends, but his father passed away and he had to take over the family business, which took him away for many years with only short jaunts back to America. Unfortunately, not enough time to properly court me where we could be married. We never forgot one another, and we would write occasionally. Neither of us married, feeling maybe one day we could. You might say we felt destined for each other."

I interrupted, "You said, 'was a man' and 'who had courted me,' what does that mean?"

"I will get to that in a moment. Child, when he came back to America to stay, he requested a visit. Instantly, our old familiar flame began to burn where we decided to begin our courtship. We felt like youngsters again, making plans for the future of marriage, and homes, and travels. Your parents knew about this, but until the wedding was set to take place, they did not want to tell you. Well, we set a date, which was to be May 16th, 1841, just last year. As a wedding present, a few months before our wedding, he sat for a daguerreotype to give to me. On the eve of April 16th, one month before we were to be wed, he gave that daguerreotype to me; additionally, he brought dozens of roses filling my parlor full of the sweetest scent and deepest red representing his love and passion. He said by giving this to me, he would always be connected to my heart forevermore. *Nevermore*, would I be alone." Aunt Sarah stopped walking and paused for just a moment.

"Auntie, what happened?" I nervously questioned.

"Annabel, that very night he gave me the daguerreotype, we sat in the parlor together. I was embroidering while he read his own poetry to me," she turned, locked eyes with me, grabbed both of my hands with hers, and finished, "And…and…out of nowhere, he coughed. He coughed again, a little harder as he took his handkerchief out. On the third cough, he held that handkerchief to his mouth. I did not think anything of it and kept embroidering, but on that third cough, I stopped, looking up, because it sounded as if his lung was being regurgitated out of his mouth. I ran over to him as he lifted the handkerchief from his mouth to reveal blood staining that fragile stark white fabric bearing his initials as if the reaper himself stamped my beloved's death sentence.

"Our wedding day was still planned; nothing had changed except the consumption brewing in his lungs twisting and turning the life right out of him. Annabel, he died three weeks later. That daguerreotype, his handkerchief, and his poems are the only remnants I have left of him. You might remember me going on a trip last year for around two months. I sailed on a ship to Europe to escape my thoughts of living here without him. The trip was to relieve my grief. I will never get over this; therefore, I am content to keep living with the memories of the few years we had together before death crept up too soon. He is buried in our town's cemetery. At least once a week, I visit his grave and place the same type of deep red roses to honor our love. To make sure I would always have access to that type of rose, I had a rosebush of that variety planted in my own garden." She stopped sharing, but never took her eyes from mine.

"I am so sorry Auntie. I am so sorry you had to go through this severe loss." I said as I hugged her tight, blubbering tears of sadness for her.

"Thank you, my child, having you visit me from time to time helps me so much. I do enjoy your company." Sarah said as she wiped her tears away. "Annabel, you are so young and have so many years to experience a love like mine. Promise me, if you do find this, please do not hesitate, or wait, take hold of that passion, and never let it go. I don't want to see you robbed of what I could have had."

"I promise." I answered with fingers crossed. This scared me! To think of being so close to a person and then, in one instant, he is gone, never to return. I had Auntie, and I had my parents; that was all I would ever need. I am also only fifteen years old. I am only in the springtime of my life. Who knows what life will bring? All I know is now, and everything circling my purview feels like a ring of fire protecting me, but allowing me to grow into my adulthood.

We both got ourselves together and continued to walk into town. We shopped for three hours. At the second store we patroned, one of Aunt Sarah's friends asked her to attend a gathering she was having that evening. Aunt Sarah made sure it was appropriate to bring me. When her friend saw me, she hugged me and said youth attending would be wonderful. So,

Auntie bought me a new dress at the third store and a new hat at the haberdasher. We wrapped up our shopping and walked home to get ready for the party. Again, you never know what plans will arise when you stay at Aunt Sarah's. I could not wait!

Chapter 5

Aunt Sarah had allowed us to sleep a little later Sunday morning because we were at the party later than our normal bedtime. I could not believe how festive the dinner party was with all the pleasing food and agreeable music. The menu consisted of roasted beef, potatoes, carrots, peas, apples, and pudding prepared right; nevertheless, everything was grand except the peas. I politely declined them without Auntie hearing me. I always tried to be an accepting guest, yet, having peas on one's plate was like looking at the slimy eyes of a bug-eyed frog.

I walked downstairs, the house unusually quiet, so I decided to walk outside to the local newspaper printing house to buy a paper. Luckily, this did not take too much of my time, so I speedily walked back. I opened the door normally, figuring everyone would be awake, but no one greeted me at the door or called my name when the door cracked open. I went into the kitchen to see what was for breakfast when I saw Mrs. Prosper cooking. "Good morning Mrs. Prosper, has my aunt come down yet?"

"Yes, little miss, but she went back upstairs. She said she would be down at nine for breakfast. I would not disturb her." Mrs. Prosper replied.

"Oh, that is all right. It was so quiet in the house, it just seemed odd. I went out the front door without anyone hearing me. I'll just go to the parlor and read the newspaper I bought. Thank you, Mrs. Prosper."

"I will call you when breakfast is ready."

I thanked Mrs. Prosper again and skipped into the parlor, sitting down in Auntie's high back chair. I felt so grown up when I sat there. I took out my newspaper and opened it up to the middle section of the paper. That is where they had interesting articles about scientific inventions. I liked reading about those first because it was positive and made one feel hopeful about the future. This section is where I learned about daguerreotypes. As I was reading, I heard my aunt come down and go into the kitchen. It sounded like she and Mrs. Prosper exchanged a few words and then Auntie was coming in the parlor. "Good morning dear, did you sleep well?"

"Yes, I did. I couldn't find you when I woke up and walked downstairs, and so I went to get a newspaper..." I answered.

"Annabel, you did what? Did you say newspaper?" She asked alarmingly.

"Yes ma'am. Was that wrong?"

"No, no, it was not."

"I arrived home just about ten minutes ago. I always open it up to the science section first. I haven't even looked at the cover page. I know that is silly, but..." I giggled, but she interrupted me.

Aunt Sarah reacted, "Oh, that is good. I mean, that is an interesting way to read the newspaper. Most people I know start at the beginning and work their way through until the end. How amusing? So, you said you have not seen the front?"

"No ma'am. Aunt Sarah, you seem awkward this morning. You are not acting like yourself. Are you okay?"

"Um, I will be okay. I need to talk to you, but I wanted to wait until after breakfast." She mused.

"All right, if that is the case, I will continue reading. I was just about to read the front page…" I countered to her as I turned to the front page and saw the heading, "FIRE FAILS HOTEL SOUTHERBY." Just as I read this, Aunt Sarah grabbed the newspaper from me as I passed out on the chair.

Chapter 6

I awoke to find Aunt Sarah sitting at my bedside holding my hand tightly as if she were trying to pull me out of a well. "Aunt Sarah, how long was I asleep?"

"Child, this will be hard for you to hear, but you collapsed on Sunday morning. I called the doctor, and we brought you up to your room. You have been in and out of sleep for three days. Today is Tuesday."

"Wait, did my parents decide to stay longer? Are they here? Where…" I stopped as if I had *descended into a maelstrom*. Memories flooding back like waves of emotions thrashing my brain too fast for me to make sense. "My parents, where are they? What happened at the Hotel Southerby?" I queried.

"Annabel, it seems your memory from Sunday morning is coming back slowly. I need to tell you some news. Sunday morning before you woke, a messenger rode up to the house on horseback. Mrs. Prosper heard him knock on the door, finding it odd we had a visitor. Being a little disconcerted, she went and answered the door. The young man brought a letter from someone in Richmond to me. She had him wait in the parlor while she ran upstairs to wake me up to come downstairs. I quickly dressed and dashed to the parlor. He gave me the letter. I asked him to wait while I read it in case I had questions. He obliged." She paused and took the letter from her dress pocket. "Here is what the letter said," as she read it aloud to me.

Miss Clemmons,

I am grieved to write you this letter with grave news. I am the owner of Hotel Southerby, Mr. Rodman Usher. Last night, one of the beams in the kitchen fell while my cook was baking bread overnight. My hotel is quite beautiful, but it needed many repairs. The structure was in worse condition than I had known. It was as if the hotel was trying to tell me something. I apologize as I digress. When the beam fell, it knocked over a pan on the stove, which lit the wood catching fire. The blaze moved quickly and vengefully. I and only a few guests on the first floor were able to escape. The kitchen was on the other wall of the stairs where the fire climbed higher to the second floor before anyone sleeping could realize. Not only did your sister and her husband fall to the fire, but I lost my sister, Matilda, who also resided on the second floor. She refused a cellar room because she felt it was too tomblike. Everything burned and so, unfortunately, I have none of their possessions to send to you. My regards and condolences to you and your family.

Sincerely,

Mr. Rodman Usher

"Annabel, do you remember seeing the front page of the newspaper about Hotel Southerby?" She asked.

"My mind is kind of blurry, but it is coming back to me." I responded as tears started streaming down my face as I lay there in shock. This could not be happening. "No, I must be dreaming!" At that moment, Aunt Sarah took me in her arms to comfort me as I cried what felt my weight in tears until I finally fell back asleep.

The next morning, I woke up to Aunt Sarah again sitting by my bed. It was so comforting to wake up to her face knowing she wanted to take all this pain away. "Annabel, how are you feeling?"

"Numb." I stated firmly.

"My dear, you haven't eaten a thing since yesterday morning. I brought you up a tray of some of your favorite things. Please eat a little to keep up your strength. I know this has been a shock, but we will get through this together." She said softly and reassuringly.

"Thank you, I will try to eat and maybe get out of bed. If you don't mind, I would like to be alone." I petitioned.

"Yes dear, you eat, take your time, and hopefully I will see you downstairs in a little while. I am here if you need anything." Aunt Sarah offered as she closed the door behind her.

Chapter 7

Over the next few days as I put myself together over the undeniability of my parents' deaths, I mourned inside until it felt like my insides were being ripped apart. I could not have gone through this without Aunt Sarah. In my mind, I went from fifteen to fifty mentally in just a week; however, I was still just a baby learning to walk this new life.

We had their funeral the following Saturday, two weeks from the day they died. Mrs. Prosper took care of the house to be dressed in mourning as well as myself and Aunt Sarah. Many of our family and friends paid their respects at our home and at the funeral.

My aunt had them buried close to her departed beau so when she walked to the cemetery each week, she could immediately go straight to one area of her loved ones whom she cherished. We said our goodbyes at my parents' graves, which was hard for both of us. All we had left was each other. We had no other family. It felt as if *the high-born kinsmen came* and took all our loved ones away in an instant—unsympathetic and cold-hearted to our feelings. Right at this moment, I felt nothing. I knew Aunt Sarah would take care of me; I had no doubt. Standing in this cemetery with just her by my side, I felt alone.

It made me think about my future self and what I wanted to do moving on without my parents. I was not sure I wanted to love anyone else ever again. It hurt too much!

We began walking away from the graves of my parents' holding hands and weeping profusely just like professional wailers. I looked back before moving forward. I can do this! I have Aunt Sarah.

Her hand broke from mine as she moved at a faster pace toward another grave with an arched tombstone. She bent down and touched the name as she dropped a deep red rose on the ground. I caught up to her and asked softly, "Is this him?"

"Yes, it is my beloved. I miss him so, especially in moments like these."

"What a nice name…Edgar. I wish I could have met him." I said lovingly.

"You would have loved him as your uncle. As I said, he wrote poetry, and he had the best sense of humor. Um, but every now and then, he had a dark story to tell." She added mysteriously.

Chapter 8

Over the next few weeks, my aunt sorted all the legal ramifications of my parents' will and possessions, including the legality of me and what would happen next. My parents left custody with my aunt, which I was ecstatic about because there was no one else I would rather live with compared to my parents.

Aunt Sarah arranged for a tutor to come to the house to guide me in my studies. She felt it was better for me to learn one on one with a strong teacher than to attend school. Additionally, she also hired an artist to give me lessons to refine and sharpen my skills. Unfortunately, the art teacher only comes by the house twice a week; whereas, my tutor saw me every day. I guess that is what is needed to be a well-rounded young lady.

Mrs. Ewing was my regular teacher, and she was quite the organized sort. She gave me a schedule I must follow each day after she had given her lectures and lessons. She even calculated how many hours it would take me to complete my work. She gave me this after she met me and learned my skill levels in the subjects I would take. I did enjoy learning, but for me, reading stories and poems were my favorites besides my art.

Today, Mrs. Madalena would be here to impart more of her wisdom of skills and styles of art. We had been working on portraits, but I think she mentioned we would be working on landscapes today. There was a knock at the door and Mrs. Prosper quickly moved faster than I could run to open it. Mrs. Prosper greeted Mrs. Madalena with pleasantries and invited her in. She told her I would be in the parlor, but then turned around to find me standing right behind her.

"Annabel, I thought you were in the parlor. You half gave me a fright, silly girl." Mrs. Prosper said startled.

"I am so sorry Mrs. Prosper, I was just anxious for Mrs. Madalena to arrive."

Mrs. Madalena looked at me sternly, "Annabel, a proper lady waits patiently in the parlor for her guests. Do not forget that as you will be sixteen before too long."

"Yes, Mrs. Madalena. I am just excited about our lesson today. Landscapes are my favorite. I would love to show you what I have sketched." I mentioned trying to remove myself from being scolded on young ladies' proper etiquette.

"Annabel, we will get to that, but first, gather your tools and meet me out in the backyard. The day is bright and sunny, and I want you to experience painting in that element. Once I see what you have sketched, we will focus on what I think are your struggles. So, be a good girl and quickly go retrieve your things." Mrs. Madalena ordered.

We spent the first hour looking over my drawings. She asked me many questions as to why I would use certain techniques in my sketch work. The process seemed a little exhausting, but I knew this was all to help me grow as an artist. She guided me on some new techniques for sketching first. After lunch, she taught me some basic skills with oils, which I was thrilled to use. The day seemed to move swiftly, and then it was time for her to go. We said our goodbyes as she provided my task to practice before she came back next week.

My lessons kept me extremely busy for the next few months with consistent routines. Life became a pattern for me as I slowly each day felt more like my old self before my parents' death. At first, schooling was the last thing on my mind the month after they died, but now I see Auntie knew best. I felt I was thriving in my studies and making much progress in my art. I could not wait to see what the future would hold.

Chapter 9

Before I knew it, my sixteenth birthday was coming around in October. Auntie decided to have a dinner party for the occasion. She invited many of her friends. I was perusing the guest list when I realized, there were no people my own age written down. Unexpectedly, I recognized I had hidden myself away from the world. My studies became my acquaintances and my art my companions. I went into the parlor where Aunt Sarah was sitting in her favorite chair with Catty. "Auntie, may I speak to you?"

"Absolutely, Annabel, you may come to me anytime. You know that. What is it child?"

I gulped before approaching the subject, "I was just looking at the guests you have invited to the dinner party. Um…"

"Annabel, it is not polite to pause that way. Just ask me." Aunt Sarah spoke firmly.

"I am sorry, but there are no guests who are my age. Have I become a recluse?"

Aunt Sarah gave a half smile and grasped why I was acting so strange. "My dear, you have been couped up in this house with just me, Mrs. Prosper, your teachers, and Catty so long, I guess I forgot about being young. I have been inconsiderate, and I do apologize."

"Auntie, I did not mean to accuse you of anything, but I know no one my own age. I just comprehended that fact. Do you have any acquaintances who are younger, or do any of your friends have children my age? Maybe they may attend with their parents." I suggested.

"Let me worry and work on it. You do not worry yourself over this. You do need friends."

Two weeks passed and the night arrived for our dinner party. Aunt Sarah and I were in our most fancy dress. She wore a beautiful silk gown with ivory embroidery around the collar and wrists. The pattern was quite feminine and reminded me of the jasmine vines growing around the trellis of her garden entryway. The soft pastel pink of the fabric brought out her white hair pinned up with ringlets hanging in the back like grape clusters ripe for picking. I wore a navy-blue silk gown trimmed with white lace around the neck as if I wore a scrolled chocker. The lace also adorned my puffy sleeves. This was my favorite dress I owned. It was the perfect frock for the evening to celebrate my sixteenth birthday.

All the guests had arrived making up Aunt Sarah's closest friends. They were all escorted into the parlor to listen to a gentleman for whom Auntie hired to play the piano before dinner would be served. With the number of people who had shown up, I was wondering why we were not attending to our guests. "Auntie, aren't all the guests here?"

"Actually, we are waiting for one more family to arrive." She replied coyly.

"Family, don't you mean couple?" I asked ignorantly, not understanding her hint.

"Annabel, try to recognize the tone in my voice when I am trying to hint at something. The family I am referring to are great friends of mine. The family does consist of a couple, but they also are bringing their son." Just as Aunt Sarah was explaining, they arrived.

"Good evening, I would like you to meet my niece, Annabel Allan. As you know, she is my ward and lives here with me. Annabel, this is Mr. and Mrs. Richardson."

I answered shyly, "Pleased to make your acquaintance.

Mrs. Richarson replied, "Annabel it is so nice to meet you finally. We have been travelling so much, I feel as if I lost touch with Sarah," as she looked from me to Sarah, "Annabel, we would like you to meet our son, Parker."

As she said his name, he came around from behind his father to greet me. He was tall, handsome with brown hair combed neatly to the side. His eyes were clear blue like water in a fountain, but his eyes seemed to speak of something I could not understand. Maybe he was shy like me. I was willing to find out. "How do you do Mr. Richardson?"

"Very well, my lady. It is pleasing to make your acquaintance." He held his arm out for me; I hesitated to look at Aunt Sarah as she nodded for me to put my arm through his. "Shall we?"

"Thank you." I answered uncertainly as we walked into the parlor. We talked for just a few moments when Mrs. Prosper announced that dinner was served. Parker again offered his arm and escorted me into the dining room. I felt very awkward because I knew nothing about this young man. As we walked in, I looked quickly for my place card. I would be a tad angry with Aunt Sarah if she seated Parker by me. I spied my name next to hers, and realized his was on the opposite side of the table. I did not mind getting to know him, but not at my birthday dinner.

We feasted decadently for the next few hours before heading back to the parlor to listen to more music and converse the night away. Parker stayed with me most of the night, seeing we were the youngest by twenty or thirty years among all the guests. "Parker, thank you for escorting me back into the parlor. Dinner was lovely, wasn't it?"

"Yes it was Miss Allan. I was surprised my parents invited me to attend. They normally go to these types of affairs without me; however, these days I am not home as much as I would like to be." Parker offered.

"Oh, do you travel or have a job that takes you away?"

"Not a job to date. I am studying at the University of Virginia. I want to practice law."

"Parker, that sounds intriguing. I would like to hear more about it, but I know it is getting late and many of the guests are leaving." I responded innocently.

"Miss Allan, if it would be all right with you, I could ask my parents to have you over for afternoon tea in a few weeks when I return home again." Parker suggested.

"How nice. I will speak to my aunt to ensure she gives me permission."

"I am sure she will, and she will also be invited."

I added, "Wonderful. It will be nice to visit with you again. I will accompany you to the door and say my goodbyes to your parents."

I turned slightly and felt Parker grab my hand and pull me back gently. He pulled my hand up to his mouth and kissed ever so lightly. His breath was hot. I did not know how to feel at this, but I politely curtsied and said a hesitant thank you.

Aunt Sarah and I bade goodbye to all our guests and went back into the parlor to rest before going up to bed. "Auntie, thank you ever so much for this elegant party. Everyone was so sweet, and the dinner was divine."

Aunt Sarah replied, "You are welcome my darling. I was giddy to make you happy. I noticed you speaking to the Richardson boy. He is quite a charming one. He is at university. He would make a delightful husband one day."

"Um, I guess so. He was nice and we did have a nice chat; however, as we were walking toward the door, he kissed me on the hand. I was shocked; amazingly, I was not sure what to say or do." I added unsure of what her reaction would be.

"Well, what did you do?" Aunt Sarah asked with concern.

"I probably blushed, but I said thank you and curtsied. Did I do exude the correct behavior?"

"Oh, my dear, you did. It is okay to be a little coy, but never be too bold. It will get you into trouble. The type of trouble I am not ready to discuss with you yet. I know we are both tired, so let's go up to bed."

"One more thing. He asked you and I to tea at the Richardson's in a few weeks when he returns home. He said his mother would contact you."

"Lovely, I can't wait." She said putting her hand on her heart as if this news made her sentimental.

Chapter 10

The next few weeks went by rapidly. Plans had been made for tea with the Richardson's for tomorrow afternoon. There was tutoring, lessons, and art practice, which I was so thrilled about because Mrs. Madalena took me to many places in town to sketch and paint. I was growing more proficient each day and I could not be more proud of myself. Today, she said she had a surprise for me. The anticipation of her arrival filled me with such emotion, I felt like a five-year-old little girl waiting for a lollipop. "Annabel, calm down, patience is something you need to practice more often. I would be excited to because I know where you are going, and that is why I am going with you two. She will be here shortly. Do you have your things packed to work this afternoon?" Aunt Sarah asked.

"Yes, ma'am. I am ready whenever she gets here."

Just at that moment, there was a knock at the front door. I briskly walked to open it, and there was Mrs. Madalena smiling brightly. "Good afternoon, Annabel, are you ready to go?"

"Yes ma'am, I am. Let me go get Auntie."

She replied, "My carriage awaits."

We put on our coats and hats. I picked up my tools. We went out the front door to a lovely handsome and climbed in.

Mrs. Madalena even had the curtains drawn so the surprise would come when we arrived.

The travel time was noticeably short, so I knew we were not far from town, but I could hear what seemed like wind, stronger than what we always hear at Auntie's house. Before we stepped out of the carriage, Aunt Sarah took my arm. "Annabel, I know this will be a surprise when we walk outside. Once you see where we are, if you have any doubts at all about staying here, just say the word and we will leave straightaway. Do you understand?"

"Auntie, I can't imagine wanting to leave a place Mrs. Madalena has picked out for me to draw." As I said this, I stepped out of the handsome and looked around. Familiarity crept up my body like ivy crawling up an oak tree as I knew where we were instantly—my parents' home on the cliff by the sea.

I stopped for a moment to take it all in: the howling wind, the smell of the sea air, the fragrances wafting from their garden, and the beautiful home they built for eternity together. Why have I stayed away for so long? I could feel their presence here as I walked towards the garden, which remained as beautiful as when they left it. "Auntie, the garden, has someone been taking care of it?"

"They have. I hired a caretaker to live here to manage the house and grounds so one day when you were older, it would be ready for you to live in if you choose to do so."

Mrs. Madalena added, "Annabel, your aunt has taken such great care to keep this just as it was when you lived here with your parents. It is breathtaking!"

"Thank you Auntie." I said as I walked over to the cliff and gazed upon the sea. It made me feel at home, but I also felt as I was treading on a place from the past. I needed to knock myself out of this weird feeling and get to doing art. Mrs. Madalena and I chose a spot where I could look out to the sea and begin sketching a landscape. We both worked, she on a similar painting, and me on mine.

"Annabel, how about a break? I think the caretaker made some tea." She asked.

"Sounds fine. Mrs. Madalena, I must confess, I have loved being back by the ocean, but I am having a challenging time being here. My feelings are telling me I should have already come back. Looking around, I feel guilty."

"Please do not feel that way. Your parents would have wanted you to grow and thrive into the young woman you are becoming. Sarah told me how much they encouraged your art. Annabel, you are exceptionally good, and I can see your work in a gallery one day. We just need to keep working. Think of it as a tribute to your mother and father."

"I never thought of it that way. I love the idea. Will you help me?"

Mrs. Madalena responded as she walked over to me, "I will be happy to," she said as she gave me a hug. "The more you come out here the easier it will be to accept things as they are and to know your parents loved you dearly."

I countered, "I know. Again, thank you." I hugged her back and we walked up towards the house, but I indicated I wanted to walk through the garden first. "This garden was my parents' dream. They nurtured it like a baby and hoped I would grow to love it as they did. I was supposed to start painting it when the tragedy occurred." I said holding back a few tears as I noticed a rose bush terribly like the one Aunt Sarah had in her garden, but slightly more unique. I called my aunt to come outside to the garden.

"Yes, Annabel, what is it?" Aunt Sarah asked.

"This rose bush, it is so much like yours. I never even noticed how they were so close in color and size. Are they the same variety?"

"The two rose bushes are different varieties, but remarkably similar: one is darker than the other, but in shape and petal, they are quite the same. Your mother chose a blue, red rose bush and I chose a black, red rose bush." Aunt Sarah explained.

Confused, I countered, "What do you mean chose? Did you pick these out together?"

"Annabel, I forgot, and I apologize for not telling you sooner. Your mother should have already told you our family lore, but she wanted to save this for when you either turned eighteen or married, whichever came first. Our last name was Clemmons as you know. Our family dates to olden times, probably before Shakespeare. Our mother passed this down, as did her mother, and all the mothers before her. We have a coat of arms for our family crest. It is beautiful; remind me to show it to you when we go home. The focus on the crest is a rose. Each petal is a deep, deep red, but each petal also has a touch of a distinct color that has been seen in different varieties of roses. Each Clemmons female gets to choose their colors and plant a rose bush to represent their part of the family lineage. This representation gives a sense of pride and honor because all

Clemmons women are thorny and beautiful just like a rose bush. We take care of ourselves and our family heartily and diligently, but we are soft and full of love. You might say the thorns represent darkness and the flowers represent the light. When you become of age in just a few years, you will need to choose your own."

In awe, I rejoiced, "Oh Auntie, that is a beautiful story. I knew you and Mother always had a fondness for roses, but I had no idea the penchant for them was rooted in this deeply. I can't wait until I am eighteen!"

"In due time my child. Before you go off speeding up time, we need to get ready to go see your gentleman tomorrow." Aunt Sarah retorted.

Chapter 11

The next day arrived seemingly. I had mixed feelings about going to tea at the Richardson's. On one hand I was excited to see Parker again; on the other hand, I wondered how much we had in common. I guess I will never know until I spend further time with him. He was quite nice and intelligent. He came from a good family and his studies would provide a life for whomever he married. There was just a twinge in me that I was not sure. I finished pulling up my dark hair into a braided bun when I reached over to pick up my enameled comb, which was not in the place I left it. I added some hair pins so my hair would stay in place as I looked around for my comb. "I know I left it here on my vanity."

Mrs. Prosper heard me in the hallway and entered my room. "Annabel, miss, is there something a matter?"

"Actually, yes, my hair comb is missing. I left it on my vanity and now I can't find it."

"I'll help you." She offered.

We both looked around the floor, under the bed, around other pieces of furniture, and it was just missing. "Mrs. Prosper, thank you for helping me search. I must have placed it somewhere else. I will add another piece, and I'll look for it later."

Mrs. Prosper said, "Your aunt is ready to leave whenever you are ready. She is down in the parlor."

I quickly added another decorative hair pin to the top of my bun and hurried downstairs. We left immediately for the Richardson's.

The carriage ride proved to be short due to the Richardsons living close by our house. They greeted us at the door and welcomed us into their sitting room. "Annabel, Parker had to go into town, so he will be a little late. I do apologize on his part." Mrs. Richardson said.

"It is quite all right, I understand." Answering with trying not to seem too nervous at his arrival.

"Constance, didn't you say you were planning a trip soon?" Aunt Sarah inquired.

"Yes Sarah, we are going to New York City in just a few weeks. John's business takes him there and I will be accompanying him. While he works, I thought I would do some shopping. Several of the markets have beautiful fabrics I want to purchase for new drapes for the dining room. I also want to choose some new fabric for dresses I want made. I think it will be heavenly to shop there."

"I agree, New York City has some of the best shopping." Sarah added.

Mrs. Richardson and Aunt Sarah kept their conversation consistent about fabric, dress patterns, and the latest styles while I sat drinking my tea and daydreaming about when Parker would arrive. I did like shopping for new fabric, but my unhinged anticipation for what came next with Parker would not allow me to participate in their conversation. It was obvious they felt Parker and I were suited to each other, but how could they, we only met once. Did they know more than we did? Or did they just want both of us to find happiness with each other so we would be taken care of by matching us together? I am sure Auntie thought of these things, but she never really talked with be about this topic. At sixteen, marriage was the last thing on my mind. Unexpectedly, a squeaky door interrupted my thoughts.

"Good afternoon, I do apologize for my lateness. I had some errands to attend in town. I hope that everyone is having a quaint tea time." Parker greeted us with a smile.

"Ah, Parker, you are a dear. Come in and have some tea." Mrs. Richardson said invitingly.

Parker sat in the chair next to mine and addressed me cheerfully. "Hello, Miss Allan, it is so good of you to join us for tea. I have quite been looking forward to seeing you again."

"Thank you, Mr. Richardson. Your home is exquisite. May I inquire how your schooling is going at present?"

"My studies are moving very splendidly. My marks are some of the highest in my class with rhetoric as my grand achievement. I am thankful for that because I will need those skills as an attorney. What types of things have you been doing of late?"

I responded, "I have a teacher who sees me each day, so I am working on many subjects, which I enjoy; however, my art teacher, Mrs. Madalena, comes twice a week to give me lessons. My art is by far my favorite."

"Indeed, I would like to see some of your work. That is quite charming you paint."

"Thank you, Mr. Richardson."

Parker suggested, "How would you like to go out on the veranda and talk? The adults seem to be in their own conversation and won't miss us. I know my parents will not mind."

I thought for a moment and asked, "Aunt Sarah, is it satisfactory for me to accompany Mr. Richardson out onto the veranda?"

"Sarah, it is just outside the double doors behind me. They will be fine." Mrs. Richardson gestured.

"Absolutely, Annabel, go right ahead." She agreed as she could peer out through the doors to see them.

Parker bent down and offered me his arm and I acquiesced. As we moved outside, I looked around to see their property, which was gorgeous: a place I might want to paint someday. The placement of the trees, their garden, the lake, and their gazebo created a charming landscape one would dream of from a book. "This view is breathtaking!"

"It absolutely is. I enjoy coming out here to think. Sometimes I walk the grounds taking in the scenery. I also enjoy riding horses around the area. Do you like horses?"

"Actually, I have never ridden horses, Mr. Richardson. My family has only owned a horse for our carriage where our groundskeeper took care of the animal." I explained.

"Oh, please do call me Parker and I will call you Annabel. We are friends now, aren't we?" He asked supposedly.

"Yes, Annabel is fine. I guess we are friends, especially with your parents and my aunt being friends." I said hurriedly because I didn't know how I really felt at this point of our second meeting. He was quite nice, friendly, and charming. I think my nervousness was just getting hold of my emotions to be guarded. "Yes, Parker, we are friends."

"Splendid! Then, while I am home, you must come back over, and I will take you riding through the grounds."

"Okay." I said knowing I would need to ask Aunt Sarah first. Parker and I continued to talk about his studies and about horses. He was fascinating, and I could feel my guard slowly moving away little by little as I became more comfortable being around him.

As we talked, his mother came outside to say it was time for me to leave. We walked in together with my arm through his. We said our goodbyes and Aunt Sarah and I rode home in our carriage. Once home, dinner was served, and we ate a wonderful meal before settling into the parlor for a little while. Our routine of Aunt Sarah with her needlework and I with my sketching picked up just where it left off the previous evening.

I discussed with Aunt Sarah how Parker invited me to go horseback riding. She seemed to question this because it was something I had never done before, but then she thought about it and agreed to make the arrangements. A little excitement seemed to be brewing in my heart thinking about trying something new. This would be an adventure!

We both walked upstairs to go to bed. I was still elated with this new feeling as I went into my bedroom to begin taking down my hair. I sat at my vanity to do that and began brushing my hair when I noticed the comb I looked for earlier was staring right at me dead center on my vanity. This was odd! I thought for a moment and then dismissed this as maybe Mrs. Prosper found it and laid it here. That was thoughtful of her; yet, she didn't say anything at dinner. I shooed away the weird feelings and finished dressing for bed dreaming about Parker.

The following week I was getting ready for my visit with Parker to begin learning how to ride a horse. I was both nervous and ecstatic all at the same time. I hurried downstairs to find Mrs. Prosper's daughter, Jane, who was taught at a youthful age how to ride horses. She would accompany me as my chaperone for the day. We left in our carriage to travel to the Richardson's house for an adventure I would never forget.

As soon as we arrived, Parker's mother called him down for pleasantries before we walked out to the stable. Mrs. Richarson seemed happy to see me arrive with a smile on my face. I knew she and Aunt Sarah were conniving about Parker and me. Parker escorted us to the stable where he had his stable hand ready with the horses. Jane and Parker discussed many things I needed to know before I even climbed up on the horse, especially since I was riding side saddle. My mind seemed overwhelmed, but I paid close attention to their instructions.

They helped me move up onto the horse, a beautiful grey and black mare who was calm seeming to know I had never done this before. "Annabel, are you ready?" Parker asked excitedly.

"As ready as I will ever be." I returned.

Just like that, we three began to ride slowly. Parker took me around the garden area first, which was created as a maze with differing plants, flowers, and trees at every turn. If the maze were taller, I would never find my way out if I were by myself. After the maze, we trotted through the pathway through many trees, which rounded us by the lake. As we moved close to the water's edge, I noticed several pine and oak trees surrounding the lake, which created dark shadows around the surrounding area. It felt lonely here because through the trees, the area seemed overgrown and unkempt. Only the small area we rode to was clear. There were many areas where there were algae covered rocks stacked upon each other at the water's crest. Some of the rocks looked black, but that might just have been the shadows playing tricks with my light blue eyes. With all this dreariness, the lake was picturesque—a place I wanted to paint.

"Annabel, what do you think of my lake?" Parker asked.

I replied, "It is a handsome lake even with all its darkness."

"I knew you would like it." He dismounted his horse and came over to me to help me down. Jane brought over a picnic basket and a few blankets for us to sit and have a little dinner and break from riding. "As a boy, I rode over here almost every day. I loved to sit and think about games I liked to play and what I wanted to do. I also skipped rocks and searched for "buried treasure" as I played pirate. Now, I come here to think if I am working on a lesson, I am having trouble with. The peace and quiet suits me, even though I mostly enjoy being around lots of people; I still need a little quiet time."

"That is nice you have a place to contemplate. When you are mostly with others, it is hard to find those quiet spots sometimes." I added cheerfully.

Once we ate and talked some more about Parker's plans for when he finished at university, he helped me up on my horse again. As he did, he held my hand lingering there and staring into my eyes. It was a nice feeling. Straightaway, we rode back to his house and put the horses back in the stable. All three of us walked back to the house for some tea. Parker's mother came into the sitting room and asked Jane to come into the kitchen. I had a feeling Parker had his mother do this so we could be "almost" alone, at least alone enough where there was not a guard seated right at the cell door. "Annabel, did you enjoy yourself today?"

"Yes, I enjoyed this more than I believed I would. Thank you for teaching me this today."

"You are quite welcome. You did fine for your first ride. We will need to have you practice some more." He suggested as he took my hand and kissed the top part again like he did the first night I met him. His lips pressing down on my skin caused tingles all over me. I know I blushed, and I felt embarrassed. "Annabel, I will be going back to school at the end of the week. I want to continue seeing you on all my visits home. Will you write to me?"

"Yes Parker, of course. I would like very much to exchange letters with you and to see you again. I think your mother and my aunt wish that as well."

Parker added, "I am so pleased you agree. Yes, I think they are little matchmakers at work like busy little bees. I think their stingers worked with us, but the sting is not painful, it feels boundless where this relationship could grow." As he said this, he kissed my cheek tenderly without hesitation. I felt so elated that I would faint, but I just smiled ever so. He seemed to want to kiss me on the lips, but Jane and Mrs. Richardson came back into the sitting room.

"Annabel, it has been a lovely afternoon, but I think it is time we said goodbye. I promised your aunt I would have you home well before dinner." Jane interrupted.

"Yes Jane." We stood up from the settee and Parker walked me to the carriage.

"Parker, thank you for such a wonderful day. I look forward to seeing you again."

"I as well, my dear Annabel. I will be home in a few weeks, and I will call on you. For now, we will write to each other. It was an honor to be in your company today. I wish you well and I look forward to seeing you on my next visit home." Parker said as he kissed the top of my hand as he helped me into the carriage.

I swooned, but kept my composure on the ride home. Parker had a charismatic quality about him that is irresistible. I looked forward to getting to know him more.

We arrived home before I even realized because I was reflecting on our day together. I greeted Aunt Sarah before going upstairs to change into my dinner attire. As I was pulling out my dinner frock, I was standing in front of my vanity mirror, which faced the wall where my little desk sat. I sit here quite often reading or writing letters. I noticed one of my poetry books was open. I thought to myself how odd. I never leave books open because I do not want to crease the spine. I took great care of my things. I put on my dress, and I walked over to my desk. Looking down, I gathered that it was my poetry collection by Edgar Allan

Poe. In further study, I saw that the page the book was opened to was on the poem, *The Lake*. As I buttoned my dress, I read the poem aloud.

In youth's spring, it was my lot
To haunt of the wide earth a spot
The which I could not love the less;
So lovely was the loneliness
Of a wild lake, with black rock bound.
And the tall pines that tower'd around.
But when the night had thrown her pall
Upon that spot — as upon all,
And the wind would pass me by
In its stilly melody,
My infant spirit would awake
To the terror of the lone lake.
Yet that terror was not fright —
But a tremulous delight,
And a feeling undefin'd,
Springing from a darken'd mind.
Death was in that poison'd wave
And in its gulf a fitting grave
For him who thence could solace bring
To his dark imagining;
Whose wild'ring thought could even make
An Eden of that dim lake.

This was such a hauntingly beautiful poem, bittersweet and melancholy ruled the words Mr. Poe had written. I walked over to my vanity and smoothed my hair as I kept going over some of the lines: *Of a wild lake, with black rock bound. And the tall pines that tower'd around.* Hmm, something seemed familiar. I repeated these lines over and over and recognized Parker's lake fit this description. Surprised of the coincidence, I smiled inwardly. Before heading downstairs, I paused at my desk to read the poem again. One of the words struck me this second reading—terror. I kept reading, coming to the lines: *Springing from a darken'd mind. Death was in that poison'd wave/And in its gulf a fitting grave.* As I finished the rest of the poem, it gave me chills. Did I leave this book open? Come to think of it, I haven't read anything out of Poe's poems in a few weeks. What was going on?

At dinner, I still felt uneasy. I continued running scenarios in mind trying to figure out how that book was open and how that poem had so many elements of the lake at Parker's house. I needed to stop this nonsense, or I would go mad. The logical explanation was to ask Aunt Sarah if she had been in my room looking for a book. "Auntie, have you by chance been in my room today?"

"Oh dear, no. I tend to ask you before going into your room."

"I do not care if you go in my room. Are you sure you weren't looking for a book to read?"

Sarah adamantly added, "Annabel, I have been reading a novel for the past few weeks when I have had time to read. I will not be looking for a new book for a while. What's the matter? I can tell you are keeping something."

"It is probably just rubbish, but when I came home rushing upstairs to dress for dinner, my Edgar A. Poe poetry collection was open to the poem, *The Lake*. I haven't looked at that book in some weeks, but it was open on my desk. What do you make of that?"

"I think it sounds like you forgot about reading in it, maybe last night and you left it open when I called you for dinner, or maybe even breakfast this morning. You have had an exciting day today. It is easy to forget trivial things like leaving a book open. I would not worry too much over it." Aunt Sarah added dismissively.

We finished dinner and I decided to adjourn to my bedroom early because I was exhausted from the excitement from the day. I sat down at my vanity brushing my hair still thinking about the book. By happenstance, I looked at my combs and my favorite one stood out. Wait, the comb! The opened book was just like the missing comb. None of it made sense. Or was I seeing things that were not there?

Chapter 12

The following few weeks went by slowly like waiting on Christmas day to arrive. Just as promised, Parker called upon me. During this visit, we went horseback riding several of the days, we dined together in the company of one of our family members of course, and we grew closer. Close enough, that parting from him now was extremely difficult and a challenge. It seemed he was feeling the same way. Could this be love? I wasn't sure yet, but I felt something strong for him. My confidence grew each time we saw each other, but there was still a semblance of a question that lay in my brain. I normally eschewed it to my youth and inexperience in courting as I eschew these thoughts now.

Unfortunately, he ventured back to school until he could return the following month. His letters would keep me warm at night while he was away.

I had forgotten about my mysterious comb and book incidents until the week after Parker went back to school. In my bedroom, I was up late reading. Everyone in the house slept silently in the dark recesses of their rooms where the house kept all the sounds to itself like a selfish child with a new toy. I put my book down and decided to go downstairs to find a little something to eat. I knew Mrs. Prosper had leftover bread laid out on the kitchen counter to use for breakfast the next morning. I lit a candle and crept surreptitiously down the stairs not to wake anyone. I found the bread and cut a slice as well as pouring a small glass of milk. Enjoying my little snack for just a moment, I looked out at the night skies. Oh, how exquisite they were. There was a full moon out, but the sky was also filled with fluffy, yet menacing clouds. Maybe those clouds would bring me dreams as I thought of Parker.

Finishing, I cleaned up after myself before going back to bed. While I turned to cover the bread up, I felt a chilling wind breeze across my back as the kitchen window slammed open blowing out my candle like a tornado. I could not see very well except for the moonlight shining in. Shutting the window was easy with the moonlight smiling at me as a friend. Walking quietly and carefully, I found my candle and hugged the wall finding my way to the hallway leading to the accessible area to the stairs. My little flint was upstairs so I could not relight my candle. I knew the house well enough to find my way in the dark. As I began the ascent to the second floor, I happened to look up. Before me was an ethereal being pointing to the front door. I turned to look, just seeing the door *and nothing more*. I flashed back around, and again, there was nothing there. The darkness must be tricking my eyes. However, I felt as though someone or something was with me—a presence I should not fear. At this eerie feeling, I began to run up the rest of the stairs rapidly to my bedroom, shutting the door without looking back. I crept under my covers all the way up over my head. Should I keep this to myself or tell Aunt Sarah? I decided, for now, I would keep this a secret. What I saw must have been my imagination. If I tell Auntie, she will worry too much. At that decision, I fell fast asleep.

The next morning, I woke up continuing my normal routine and headed down for breakfast. I greeted Aunt Sarah and Mrs. Prosper and sat down. "Annabel, you usually greet Gordon when he brings the newspaper. You must not be quite awake yet." Aunt Sarah said as she teased me.

"Silly Auntie, I am awake. I just forgot. I have other things on my mind lately." I responded as I got up from the table heading to the front door. Before I reached for the doorknob, I felt a cold chill, seemingly like the one last night in the kitchen. Upon touching the knob, it felt hot like a stoked poker from the fire place. My hand jumped back from the heat. I looked around the room, but everything was in its usual place. I convinced myself I was acting like a little school girl. I reached out again, and the knob felt normal. I hurriedly turned and opened the door. Gordon was not there yet, which made me look down for some odd reason. On the front stoop, was the newspaper. Gordon must have left it earlier. Walking out, I bent down and grabbed it. Looking further down on the next step down, I noticed there was a bouquet of dead roses tied with a black ribbon. I screamed!

"Annabel, what's wrong?" Aunt Sarah yelled while running to the front door.

"Look!" I yelled back pointing at the step.

Aunt Sarah reached down and picked up the ghastly dreadful bouquet. "Oh my, where did this come from? Annabel, it is okay. Let's go inside."

We walked back in and went to the dining room. Aunt Sarah had Mrs. Prosper bring breakfast, thinking it would help me to calm down. We ate and she calmed me down saying Gordon must have found it in the yard and he just put it there to dispose of it later. She told me she would talk to him. She also reminded me Mrs. Madalena was coming today for an art lesson. This cheered me up.

Mrs. Madalena arrived, and we began working immediately in the backyard. My art always distracted me from anything, good or bad, I had on my mind. I delved into my own world when I was sketching, drawing, or painting. Out of the corner of my eye, I saw Gordon going around the house to the front. A few minutes later, I saw him in the kitchen window talking to Auntie. I asked Mrs. Madalena if she wanted something to drink, and luckily, she did. I went in through the back door as quiet as a mouse so I could hear Aunt Sarah's and Gordon's conversation. If there was anything strange about that bouquet, I feared she would keep it to herself. I listened stealthily.

"Miss Clemmons, I tell you, I didn't put them dead flowers on the step. When I ran out to get your paper, I come right back and placed it on the stoop. Not a 'nother thing was there. Promise to the saints above. Please believe me. I'd ne'er lie to you, ma'am." Gordon said.

"Gordon, I believe you. I've known you for too long to know if you were lying to me. How could it have ended up there?" Aunt Sarah quizzed.

"I'd say the wind."

At that, Aunt Sarah dismissed Gordon back outside and went about her business. I walked into the kitchen and poured tea for Mrs. Madalena and myself. I just kept thinking about this. The wind?"

Chapter 13

Parker arrived home a few weeks later, making it the longest month I've ever waited on. As he came into town, he stopped by my house before going home to surprise me. Mrs. Prosper answered the door and showed him into the parlor. I looked up when she entered and cleared her throat. "Parker!" I said as I rushed over to him. He grabbed me and hugged me and then we sat down.

"Annabel, I'm so happy to see you. Tomorrow night, I will pick you up around six o'clock. Wear your fanciest dress and be prepared for an enchanting evening."

"How lovely! Will I see you later this evening?" I asked.

"Unfortunately, no. That is why I stopped before going home. I need to get there to unpack and then I have a few things to attend to. Remember, be ready at six tomorrow evening."

"I will." I added as he kissed me on the forehead and headed out the door.

Aunt Sarah looked at me and smiled. "My goodness, you would think he would have taken a breath in between sweeping you off your feet and going home."

At that, we both laughed. I asked her to go upstairs so we could pick out my dress and accessories for tomorrow night. He made it seem like a special occasion, so I wanted to look my absolute best. We spent a few hours going through my things until we decided on my pale pink silk dress. It brought out the natural pink in my cheeks and lips and complemented my brunette hair and pastel blue eyes.

The next afternoon arrived faster than I could count. I could not contain my nerves. As I was laying out my dress and other items, my mind went to a dark place. I picked up the comb and began thinking of the three odd occurrences: the missing comb, the opened book, and the bleak bouquet. Did these three things have a commonality or were they just coincidences? Rationally, they were just pure chances; however, if they were related, they must be some kind of omen. I told myself, "Annabel, get this out of your mind!" Unfortunately, I couldn't because when I thought about the ethereal being on the stairs, I just now fathomed it looked like my mother.

Chapter 14

Six o'clock was arriving before I could believe. I calmed my nerves about the realization, I might be haunted by the spirit of my mother by drinking some chamomile tea and taking a nap. I had to come to reality; I had hallucinated, and I must now act like a grown-up. My aunt helped me get ready and she helped me with my hair. I glided down the stairs with glee as it was fifteen minutes before Parker would arrive.

The knock on the door made my heart race. Aunt Sarah answered the door and called for me to come into the foyer. "Annabel, you are stunning," Parker admired as he kissed my cheek., "Miss Clemmons, I will safely have her back at an early hour."

"Thank you Parker. You two have a magnificent evening." Aunt Sarah said as she glowed. I spied a little tear in the corner of her right eye.

The carriage took us swiftly to his parents' house where we were greeted by them most graciously. We visited with them to catch up on what I had been doing with my art and lessons while Parker was at school. Their cook announced dinner about thirty minutes later, so we dined and talked some more. After dinner, we went back into the sitting room. Parker excused himself to go check on something.

He stayed gone for about fifteen minutes while I spoke with his parents. Suddenly, Parker returned, "Annabel, how about we go out to the veranda? It is a lovely evening."

"I would like that." He put my arm in his and we went outside. As we went through the door, I saw several candles lit and there were beautiful bouquets of mixed flowers all around me. It smelled sweet like a perfumery. "Parker, what is all this? It isn't my birthday or some other special occasion." I said as I twirled around looking at the beauty he had put forth.

I turned around and he was down on one knee. "Sweet Annabel, I know we have never said we loved each other, but I know we do. I still must finish school, but I don't want you to find someone else while the university pulls me away from your loveliness. Would you do me the honor of becoming my wife?"

As he spoke, he had placed my hands in his looking up at me with those clear blue eyes I could not resist. All thoughts went out of my head as I answered him, "Yes, Parker, I will."

He jumped up, hugged me, and gave me my first kiss. It felt nice as if he knew what he was doing, making me feel protected. He was gentle, but I could tell he wanted to add more passion like he was holding back for my sake. "Annabel, you have made me the happiest man alive. I have something for you." As he said this, he pulled a ring from his pocket. "I found this ring and I knew it had to be meant for you, my love. It is a sapphire, but a very dark sapphire. It reminded me of the color you wore the first time we met. I do love you."

I accepted the ring, "Parker, thank you, it is the most beautiful ring I have ever seen. I love you, too." We hugged and kissed again. He stood behind me holding me as he cradled his arms around me as we looked deep into the sky with the brilliant stars congratulating us as they twinkled. We stayed on the veranda for quite a while talking about how happy we were. As the night created a chill, we decided to go inside.

"Father and Mother, I am pleased to announce Annabel Allan accepted my proposal." Parker announced.

"Son, that is wonderful!" Mr. Richardson said happily.

"Oh, Parker and Annabel, I am so happy for you both. Come here!" Mrs. Richardson joyfully reacted.

They both hugged me and Parker. We stayed a little longer and then it was time to take me home. When we arrived, Parker escorted me in as Aunt Sarah met us at the door. "Well, do either of you have some news?" She said obviously knowing what Parker had been up to.

"Yes, Miss Clemmons. We are engaged to be married. Annabel accepted." Parker added.

"Oh, how brilliant! I knew she would." Aunt Sarah hugged both of us. She went back to the parlor as I was making my goodbyes to Parker.

"My dear, I will see you tomorrow. I know our wedding will be belated, but the time will fly until you are my bride." He kissed me, a little harder this time and I could feel it down to my toes."

"I am a very patient lady. I will see you tomorrow." I exclaimed as I shut the door.

Chapter 15

Each day arrived as a promise of marriage came closer and closer to the time of our wedding. Every few weeks, Parker would come home. We spent every minute we were allowed to spend together riding horses, talking, and making plans. He would talk about college life as he was involved in boxing and other sports. He was a man's man, extraordinarily strong and confident. I showed him my art and he always complimented me on my work, but he did not like attending gallery shows, so I saved those to attend with Auntie and Mrs. Madalena. I really wanted to share poetry books with him, but he was not as sentimental as I was. He treated me like a queen, I feeling loved. Since I told myself to stop thinking about my odd happenings and hallucinations, I had not had anything happen I felt was off-putting. This made me grateful.

When he was away at school, we continued our letter writing. The letters kept me company while I waited for him to come home. My studies and art lessons also kept me busy where I continued to improve my art skills. Mrs. Madalena said I was almost ready to have a showing of my own. She wanted to wait until I was eighteen, however.

Time passed by like a leap frog on a never-ending path of frogs to jump over. Before I knew it, seventeen jumped over the months coming closer to eighteen with just six months from my birthday.

It was Easter and Parker had come home once more. He was in a cheerful mood. "Annabel, I don't want to wait much longer for our wedding. How about we set a date?"

"Parker, this seems so sudden because I thought we were going to wait until I was eighteen. It is only a few months."

"I can't wait, so when do you want to marry me?"

"My aunt and I might need a little time to plan the wedding, at least a few months. What about a date in June?" I explained.

"June sounds perfect. I know I still have a year to finish school, but after we are married, you can stay with my parents until I finish. How about June 29th?"

"I think that is a splendid day!" I called out as I kissed him.

We told Aunt Sarah and his parents about when we wanted to wed. They gave us our blessing with Aunt Sarah, Mrs. Richardson, and I beginning the plans.

From the end of April until the beginning of June, I was a busy bee. I was planning my wedding, working on my art, and filling in time with Parker when he was home. "Auntie, are you still coming with me to look at flowers?"

"I was planning on it, but did you hear the door just a bit ago? That was a messenger. The young man brought me a note to meet Mrs. Richardson as soon as I could."

"Oh, I am sure it must be something about the wedding. I'll go look at flowers while you go to the Richardson's. When I am finished, I will just come home."

Aunt Sarah agreed, "Perfect idea. I will see you shortly."

I went to look at flowers, which were all so amazing. I had a tough time thinking of what to choose, but I finally made the decision of white roses with delphiniums. I wanted something blue to go with Parker's eyes. As soon as I finished, I went right home. When I walked through the door, I heard Aunt Sarah speaking with someone. In the parlor were she and Mr. and Mrs. Richardson. I felt something off based on their facial expressions, but I quickly attributed this to the excitement of the wedding. "Annabel, please come and sit next to me." Aunt Sarah requested as I moved slowly watching Mrs. Richardson as she put her handkerchief up to her eyes.

"Auntie? Mrs. Richarson? What's wrong?"

"Annabel, I need you to keep calm while I tell you something." I couldn't take my eyes off Mrs. Richardson. "Please focus on me," she grabbed my hands and continued, "Mr. Richardson received a message early this morning. That is why they summoned me to their house. It seems Parker was in an accident. He…"

I interrupted. "Accident? Where is he? Is he okay?"

"Annabel, please be brave. He was walking down an alley on his way home. He had gone into town last night after school," she paused as she took a moment to gain her composure, "a man jumped out from behind some crates and shot him."

I lost all self-control and began crying profusely. "Aunt Sarah, where is Parker?"

"My very precious dear child, Parker died last night from the gunshot wound." Aunt Sarah calmly stated and held me as I cried until I passed out.

Chapter 16

I woke up in my bed unknowing what day it was. Aunt Sarah right by my side. I was having déjà vu from the remembrance of my parents' death just a few years before. "Good morning, sweet child. I am here for whatever you need."

"Auntie, what day is it?"

"You have been in bed for about two days. Do you remember why?"

"I do," I began to cry, "it wasn't a dream, was it?"

"No, my dear, Parker is gone I am so sorry to say. His funeral is tomorrow. I am hoping we can get you the strength to attend."

"I must attend. I was in shock, and I am still in shock. Why would anyone want to shoot him?"

"Annabel, the police are working on his case as we speak. We hope to know something soon."

"Thank you, Auntie! I do not know what I would do without you."

"I feel the same about you. I will always be here for you." Aunt Sarah said as she kissed my forehead and prompted me to try and get up to come downstairs for breakfast.

I mustered up my strength to be alert the rest of the day to be prepared for the funeral the next day. I tried to focus on Parker's loving ways thinking about the times we shared horseback riding and talking. Of all these memories, that is all I could remember us doing. I need to focus on these things later when my mind is not racing with emotions. I had an odd feeling, however. Before dinner, I went upstairs to put something in my room when I noticed the Poe poetry book was open again on my desk. This can't be! I looked on the page to see the following poem:

A Dream

In visions of the dark night
I have dream'd of joy departed —
But a waking dream of life and light
Hath left me broken hearted:
And what is not a dream by day
To him whose eyes are cast
On things around him with a ray
Turn'd back upon the past?
That holy dream — that holy dream,
While all the world were chiding,
Hath cheer'd me as a lovely beam
A lonely spirit guiding:
What tho' that light, thro' storm and night
So trembled from afar —
What could there be more purely bright
In Truth's day-star? —

I read it and the line that stuck with me was *A lonely spirit guiding*. I really did see the spirit of my mother. She has been guiding me all this time. So, what were the things she was trying to tell me? Was it protection or was it an omen? About Parker? Maybe it was as simple as she would watch over me like a guardian angel. I must believe that is true and not the other dreadful notion.

The next morning arrived as I descended the stairs dressed in my mourning clothes, the same dress I wore to my parents' funeral. I knew this was going to be one of the hardest days of my life, but I also knew with Aunt Sarah by my side, I could withstand anything.

The funeral was more difficult than I dreamed, but I held it together as the dutiful fiancé. I placed a black, red rose from my aunt's garden onto his coffin symbolizing our love. Leaving this flower felt like a beautiful, natural gesture to give, but it also felt artificial. Parker never brought me flowers, so we did not have a floral connection like Auntie described when she was engaged to her Edgar. Was I missing something?

As we were walking to the carriage, I saw a white raven perched on his coffin. I had never seen this creature before. I felt its eyes peering into the brightness of my eyes, maybe even into my soul. The fiend croaked what seemed like some type of sentiment to me and flew away as if it was *nevermore*. I began to cry again as Auntie put me in the carriage as we headed home.

Chapter 17

Almost four months passed as I tried to work through my grief and the unknown factors of who shot my fiancé. The police were still working on the case. To help with this, Aunt Sarah had Mrs. Madalena come to the house three days a week to keep me focused. Some of the time, I fully engaged in my art while other times, I just sat in front of the canvas staring into the white abyss with no creative juices flowing. Mrs. Madalena provided so much patience and understanding, not pushing me too much. She gave me little nudges and ideas to help me get back into it.

My eighteenth birthday was coming up in just a few weeks. I should be feeling the epitome of happiness, but all I could think about is the supposed situation that could never be, a newly wed bride in utter bliss. Wearing the colors of mourning did not help with this, but I would have to endure this for quite some time.

After dinner, I decided to do some reading in the parlor to take my mind off Parker. My aunt was at her desk going through some papers trying not to disturb me. As we were in our own little worlds on engagement, there was a sudden knock on the door. Mrs. Prosper went to open it. We heard her talking with someone, which sounded like a female voice. Mrs. Prosper came into the parlor to ask if we would see a young lady.

"Mrs. Prosper, did she give her name?" Aunt Sarah asked.

"No ma'am. She just said she must see Miss Annabel right away."

I looked up from my book and turned to Aunt Sarah with mystery in my eyes. I was not expecting anyone at all. Aunt Sarah returned the gaze back to me and nodded to Mrs. Prosper to bring the young lady into the parlor.

As the stranger walked in, she was holding a small bag in front of her as if it were a small valise for travel. Mrs. Prosper led her to a chair she could sit down in, and she placed the bag on the floor beside her. "I do apologize for this intrusion, but I must talk to a young lady by the name of Annabel." She said unsurely as if this might not even be the right residence.

"I am Annabel, Annabel Allan. Who might you be?"

"My name is Leonore, Lenore Whitby. Again, I am sorry about this unexpected visit. I have traveled from Charlottesville, VA and I must speak to you at once."

"Miss Whitby, do pray tell us what you have to say. I am Annabel's aunt." Aunt Sarah added.

"I traveled all this way to tell Annabel I am about to go to the police because I know who killed Parker." Lenore said bluntly.

"What? How do you know?" I asked with a start.

"Miss Annabel, I am a barmaid at the local tavern in Charlottesville. Parker frequented it several days a week while he was at school. I grew to know him well and I thought he was such a nice young man." Lenore paused and looked down.

"Please do go on with what happened."

"Well, I am not sure what he told you about his extra activities he did outside of school to pass the time. I'm not trying to start any trouble now. I just wanted to tell you first. I met Parker about two months after he started at the university. He came into the tavern to have a few ales from time to time. He then made it more of a habit frequenting the tavern almost every night. Naturally, we became friends. He not only began to come in to have ales, but he started gambling with a group who played cards in the tavern. I'm not sure if his parents even know."

I asked, "How does this have to do with his death?"

"I'm gettin' there. My brother was one of the guys he played cards with and well, uh, Parker see, got into a slight problem with money. That was just the first part of what happened."

"I can't believe this! There never seemed to be any issues or nervousness he had when he came home. You must be making this up!"

Aunt Sarah stepped in, "Annabel, calm down and let her finish her story. I also want to know why you are addressing him as Parker, a familiar way to address a young man."

"Ma'am, I'm not a lady like the two of yous. Remember, I'm a barmaid, so we get familiar with the young men who come in, so we get paid well because we can serve them more drinks. I mean nobody harm. The reason I came here 'cause I seen Parker's and Miss Annabel's notice in the newspaper that they were getting married. It was a downright shock to me because

Parker didn't mention he had a girl back home. He acted like he was as free as a daisy. About six months after I met Parker, I thought I was his girl. He took me to dinner from time to time. He was just so sweet. He brought me pretty things like hair combs, poetry books, and flowers. Every time, they were the prettiest white roses you ever did see. He finally told me when he finished school he would make me a proper wife and bring me home to his parents. So, we became remarkably familiar, as you say, with each other. I was his betrothed, so I gave myself to him."

I felt as though I was in a dream. This could not be happening. Aunt Sarah came over to the settee and put her arm around me. "Miss Whitby, so how does this tie into Mr. Richardson's death?"

"Well, Parker was already in trouble with my brother because of money he owed him, but I was able to talk my brother into waiting to do anything because Parker and I was getting married soon, or so I thought. That was when I seen the notice. I had left it on my bed because I cried the night before about it. My brother went into my room and seen it. He was furious! He came over to the tavern and pulled me out back to question me. I told him I had no idea about this Annabel lady. I got so mad I threw a bottle at him, but it missed him. I fell in the alley crying something awful. My brother came over to console me and that's when I told him the news." Lenore added.

"What news?" I asked, not knowing I wanted to hear the answer.

"The news that Parker and I were goin' to have a baby." She said nonchalantly.

I was in utter shock! This can't be my Parker. I had to keep my composure to hear the rest of her story.

"When I blurted this out, my brother, already angered with Parker about the money, and now making me look like a harlot, ran off saying 'I'll fix him!' You can bet I was scared to death! I tried to stop crying and to fix my face before I went back into the tavern. What I didn't know was Parker had come in the front door and was sitting at the bar with an ale. I went over to him, and he could tell I had been crying. He tried to get me to tell him what was wrong, but I told him later, not here. I was worried about my brother going to look for Parker. An' I was right to worry because about thirty minutes later, he shows up and drags Parker to the back alley to confront him. I ran after both. My brother demanded the money right then and then he started telling Parker about me and the baby. Parker looked at me with shock in his eyes! He asked me why I didn't tell him. My response was I had just discovered it to be the situation. My brother leapt at him, and they began to fight on the ground. They both finally got up, but my brother changed the rules—he pulled a gun out. He shot Parker without blinking and ran off with the gun. I went to Parker and held him until there was no life left." Lenore finished with tears streaming down her face before she pulled out a handkerchief.

"Miss Whitby, you must go to the police immediately. I know it is your brother, but Parker did not deserve the end he received." Aunt Sarah strongly suggested as she still consoled me.

"I know ma'am. Before Parker died, he told me to come to you, Sarah Clemmons, and Annabel Allan. He said you would help me."

Aunt Sarah responded, "The first thing we need to do is contact the police and have them meet us at Parker's parents' home. I will go with you."

"Thank you, ma'am. Annabel, I am so sorry to bring this to you. I think we were both shocked by Parker and what he did. I hope you don't hold this against me. He took advantage of both of us."

Before Lenore said this, I was slinging daggers at her with my eyes. When she said Parker took advantage of both of us, I happened to look through the door to the foyer because I just didn't know if I could keep looking at her. I saw that same ethereal figure looking at me as if imparting wisdom into my soul. At that moment, I realized he did take advantage of both of us. We were the victims here. Neither one of us knew about the other. How could Parker do this to us? "Lenore, I will also come with you and Aunt Sarah. Mr. and Mrs. Richardson, Parker's parents, I think in the long run will be incredibly happy to have a grandchild. There were some endearing qualities about Parker and hopefully, those are the qualities that will live on in your child." As I finished this sentiment, I saw my mother's spirit smile and glide away through the front door. All the last two years came flooding into my memories as I gained the knowledge today, my mother was trying to protect me from Parker. The odd occurrences were all things Parker was giving or experiencing with Lenore. I was so blind; I will never let that happen again.

Aunt Sarah searched my eyes as if what I said to Lenore was something shocking. It felt as if she was recognizing I had just grown up into a woman in just that moment. This moment of sympathy did not erase what he had done; this moment just solidified the additional grief I had to struggle through. Life was not going to be easy after this!

Chapter 18

Darkness crept everywhere around me like vines slithering as serpents intertwine paths into the crevices of the wood slats, which are spaced slanted, holding up centuries of forlorn family features of yore.

As I stand in the backyard on the eve of my birthday, I ponder what I have not completed in my youth avenging into adulthood. What is it that I yearn to attempt to satisfy my cravings of creativity? This milestone speaks to me as a mentor or muse guiding me along a curvaceous path seeking something new, something different to explore to reminisce the forgotten days of my youth merging with my future self to evolve into a redefined creature. I long to find a new craft. My heart beats loud, hearing it cacophonously makes me shudder with sensitive ears and anxious thoughts turning into my very soul.

Art, my old friend, is calling me like a cardinal calls its forever mate. I must go to the canvas and bring forth a palette anew. What will I paint? What will draw forth from my trembling mind? My thoughts are lonely now. I am alone and need respite from this emptiness. As I raise my hand to grab onto the brush, the instrument to loosen the strings to my sorrow, the vibrant colors begin to rest on the canvas coming to life as its own entity speaking to me in a language I thought I would need to translate; however, I gathered this language is something I have always known, even before the hand of death climbed into my family tree. It is an old friend, a worthy companion, I abandoned to be what seemed so long ago.

Chapter 19

The little time between when Lenore Whitby entered our existence and my eighteenth birthday came around, I swam through murky, dark waters of grief and despair not knowing how to forgive Parker, but I did. Aunt Sarah helped me by giving me time to heal not pushing me into anything but what I thought I needed for myself.

Lenore explained everything to the police about her brother. When questioned, her brother confessed, and he was arrested for murdering Parker. The Richardson's took Lenore in treating her like their own daughter and to prepare for the little blessing who would arrive some months later.

The week after my birthday, Mrs. Madalena came back to the house with some wonderful news. "Annabel, I am so happy about what I am about to tell you. I have been working with our local gallery in town showing them your work. They think you have real promise! They want to show your work."

"Oh my, Mrs. Madalena! That is exciting, but I do not have enough works for a show."

"My dear, we have six months to get ready. We have until the end of March."

"All right, I guess I need to get back to work. I hope I can muster up the inspiration to do this." I skeptically said.

Mrs. Madalena replied encouragingly, "I will be here every step of the way."

The next six months were spent sketching and painting all over town, Aunt Sarah's backyard, and my parents' home by the sea. I even convinced Auntie to allow me to do a portrait of her. When I finished it, she was quite proud. I could never have completed my paintings without Aunt Sarah and Mrs. Madalena. They not only encouraged my work, but they also brought me out of a tremendous hole of betrayal and doubt about myself into a resurgence for my passion—art.

Chapter 20

The day of my gallery show had arrived. Mrs. Madalena and the owner of the gallery, Mr. Christopher, helped place my paintings exactly right. Aunt Sarah and I finally decided to come out of our mourning attire for this event, so she had new dresses made just for the occasion. Her dress was a hunter green with a high neck and mutton chopped shoulders. She looked beautiful! My dress was exquisite. It was made with lavender silk with black lace adorned over it; the dress had sloping shoulders, and the skirt had several tiers of the same fabric.

Mr. Christopher had me stand at the entrance to receive guests where they could meet the artist. I had Aunt Sarah stand with me for support. After an hour of receiving, he told me I could go and mingle with the guests and maybe stand by some of my favorite paintings. I thought it would be fun for Auntie and me to stand next to her own portrait I completed. Aunt Sarah loved the idea; moreover, she added the effect of seeing the real Sarah versus the surreal Sarah would be an experience for any viewer.

Many guests walked by stopping to admire the painting, appreciating the real Aunt Sarah was standing by it. An older gentleman walked up and looked at the portrait for a while before he began talking with us. "How do you do young lady? My name is Augustus Wilson. Are you the artist?"

"Yes, sir, I am. My name is Annabel Allan and this is my aunt, Sarah Clemmons."

"I see the resemblance," he giggled as I giggled with him, "this is quite a likeness to your aunt. I viewed the other paintings, and it seems as though you prefer landscapes."

"I do love painting landscapes; however, I occasionally like doing a portrait every now and then. It keeps my skills in check. I focused quite strongly on landscapes for this show, but after Aunt Sarah finally agreed to sitting for her portrait, I had to include it here tonight."

"Thank you for sharing that with me. I have thought about having portraits done in the past, but never executed my own wish. I will keep you in mind for a commission in the future. Ladies, have a pleasant evening." He said as he bowed and walked away.

"Annabel, you should take commission work. It would be particularly good for your spirits. You would not be couped up in the house all the time; better yet, you would be meeting and talking to other people besides your old maid aunt, our cook, and your teacher. I know it hasn't been terribly long since the business with Parker occurred, but I am worried about you."

"Auntie, I appreciate your concern, but I will be fine. I will take into consideration doing commissions if that would make you happy."

Aunt Sarah answered imparting wisdom, "Child, it is not me who needs to be made happy; it is you!"

Chapter 21

I took my aunt's advice and with the help of Mrs. Madalena and Mr. Christopher, I was able to begin doing commissions as people asked for them. Mr. Christopher had a small room at the gallery where I could come and paint these to make it easier for clients. Working with others and making people happy did indeed make me happy. I told Aunt Sarah I had decided to just be a spinster like her. It suited her just dandy; she had her one love and so did I. Therefore, I could just live out my days living with her and Catty. Her response to this was not what I expected.

"Annabel, the love I had for Edgar was special. If he had not contracted consumption, we would be together today. I could never betray the love we had by finding someone else. You, on the other hand, did not experience this kind of love. To be blunt, Parker betrayed you like no other! He was two personalities, one for you and one for poor Miss Whitby. Unfortunately, his love for you was never genuine from the start. You are young, beautiful, and talented. You deserve to have a love like Edgar, and I shared."

"But Auntie, I am perfectly content living this way for the rest of my life."

"Annabel! With this silly talk, you are forcing me to do something I hoped you would gravitate to on your own; however, I think I need to intervene to make it happen. You will be nineteen in a little over six months, which is just two years away from your twenty-first birthday. On that day, you will receive a trust I have been managing your parents willed to you. It is what will provide you with whatever you need for the rest of your life. I was not going to tell you this until then. At that time, I was going to suggest you begin living on your own so you become more independent because I will not be around until you are old and gray. So, I am going to suggest you move into your parents' home, I will still hold your trust giving you an allowance, so you may begin your life as an adult." She sternly stated.

"Oh, Aunt Sarah, I don't want to go yet. Please. I promise I will get out more and meet people." I pleaded.

"Darling, promises are just that, plans for the tomorrows that only exist in your mind. You will be fine dear. Like I said, I will be here for you, but you must learn to fly on your own." She said this with such emotion, I knew she was right. I had to begin acting like an adult, not a petulant child.

The groundskeeper was keeping my parents' home up by Aunt Sarah's request and monetary means. She decided for us to redecorate some of the rooms to add freshness to begin living in my childhood home. She felt it would help me transition to living there. Once we had these changes completed, it would be time for me to move and she would hire a lady's maid for me who would live there with me.

Chapter 22

We spent the next year redecorating. This time with Aunt Sarah was some of my best memories with her. I felt like she was more like an older sister than my aunt, except when her authoritative tone would come out when I would revert to being sorry for myself. Aunt Sarah was also working with her attorney on the paperwork to transfer the trust over to me when I turned twenty-one, which was a little more than a year away.

I kept up with my commissions on a regular basis, but I also practiced on my landscapes as well. I saw Mrs. Madalena from time to time, not for lessons anymore, but just to visit as friends or as a mentor to a mentee.

One thing I had noticed about Aunt Sarah was how she was moving a little more slowly than she used to do. I know she was getting older, but she always had a spunk in her to match wits with me. We had a few more rooms to have painted and so we always would sit on the settee in the parlor looking at swatches of paints for the walls and fabric for the curtains. Catty would always have a paw in assisting by trying to steal a fabric swatch and escape with it.

I also noticed Catty was moving slower than usual, too. Afterall, she was around eighteen years old now. These were things I didn't want to accept, but as we all aged, I knew some things were just inevitable. Aunt Sarah and I chose the last few colors and designs. The house would be so glorious. I thought to myself how my mother would love the changes. I hoped she was proud of me. I stood up from the settee to grab my supplies because I was going to go outside and sketch this afternoon. "You go along my dear. I will walk over to the hardware store to make an order for these paints." Aunt Sarah said, but as she stood up, she coughed hard, which pushed her back down onto the settee.

"Aunt Sarah, are you okay?" I asked, putting my hand on her shoulder.

Right after she coughed, she took out her handkerchief and put it to her mouth. When she looked up, blood was on it and her bottom lip. "No, Annabel, I don't think I am."

I took her to her room to get her settled while I had Mrs. Prosper go into town to get the doctor. He apparently did not have any patients, so he and Mrs. Prosper returned swiftly. He examined Aunt Sarah thoroughly before coming downstairs with the prognosis. "Annabel, I don't have particularly good news I am sorry to say. Your aunt has consumption."

Every fiber in my being let out a squall to beat the banshees. I just slumped down with my whole face in my hands sobbing uncontrollingly. He sat down beside me putting an arm around my shoulder to console me. He just let me sob. I am sure I am not the first person he has gone through with this before.

"Annabel, it is in the initial stages, so we must have hope. Sarah is a strong lady. You just need to be there for her."

"Oh, Doctor, I will be. You shouldn't worry about that. I will just change my plans and stay here."

The Doctor retorted, "Whatever you need to do to make her comfortable."

"Thank you, Doctor. I am sure we will be seeing you soon."

The next few months brought many changes. My parents' house was finished being redecorated ready for me to move in at any time. Poor Catty died in her sleep. I found her curled up one morning next to Auntie. When I realized what had happened Aunt Sarah had already known. She said it was as if Catty called to her in the night as she passed on, which woke her up. Aunt Sarah and I wept for that sweet creature. The attorney had all the papers ready for us to sign to transfer the trust on my twenty-first birthday. He came to the house for us to finish that process. All that was left was for us to hire a lady's maid and for me to move; however, I was not leaving my Auntie.

One afternoon, Mrs. Prosper came to me to tell me about someone who she thought would be perfect for my lady's maid. "Miss Annabel, my sister was telling me her daughter was looking for work. She had been working for a family doing similar tasks I do, but the family moved out of town so they couldn't take her with them. Would you like to meet her? Her name's Miranda Rogers and she is a little older than you. I think you'd like her."

"Mrs. Prosper, that would be lovely. If you don't mind asking her to come by the house at her convenience, I would love to meet her."

The following Tuesday, Miranda Rogers came to the house to meet me. Aunt Sarah was having an incredibly good day and said she would like to meet her as well. "Annabel, I want to meet this young woman. I know if she comes from the same stock as Mrs. Prosper, she will be one heck of a companion to you. I'm feeling very well today, so help me downstairs please."

"Auntie, is that really a good idea?"

"Child, I don't care if it is or not. I insist on going downstairs. You can help me, or I'll do it myself." Aunt Sarah spouted.

I helped her downstairs and assisted her to lie down on the settee. We had other chairs for Miranda and me to sit in.

Miranda arrived a little before her appointment and Mrs. Prosper showed her into the parlor. "Miss Annabel, this here is my niece, Miranda Rogers."

"Pleased to meet you, Miss Rogers." I greeted.

"Yes, ma'am, pleased to meet you, too." Miranda replied.

Aunt Sarah said, "Miss Rogers, I am Sarah Clemmons, Annabel's aunt. I am so grateful for your coming to meet us today. Your aunt has told us some lovely things about you. What are some of the things you did working for the O'Riley family?"

"Thank you, I did the cooking, cleaning, settling the children down to bed, and any errands they needed for me to do. They were a wonderful family to work for."

"Miss Rogers, the job we are needing is working for me once I move to my parents' old home. It has been redecorated. It is located down by the sea on the high cliff. Would working for just me without the hustle and bustle of small children be all right with you?"

"Oh, please call me Miranda. Yes miss, I haven't worked for a few weeks since the O'Riley's moved, and I am so ever anxious to begin work again."

"Annabel, what say you? She sounds like the perfect fit." Aunt Sarah suggested.

"Miranda, I think you have just been hired." I said with ease in my voice relieved of finding someone to assist me.

Chapter 23

From October until March of the following year, Aunt Sarah continued to decline hanging on by withered threads. After we talked to Miranda months before, I hired her to go ahead and begin working at the house, but also assisting Mrs. Prosper here. This let me begin to get to know her, but it also gave Mrs. Prosper help. She was older than Auntie and I knew she would want to retire soon. I painted some now and then, but I couldn't take any commission because I needed to be there for Aunt Sarah. I would not have it any other way.

The middle of March arrived bringing the ides in true form. As Brutus plunged the dagger into Caesar, the consumption plunged deeper into Aunt Sarah's lungs. She looked graver and graver each day. The once strong-willed iron lady had now withered into a small fragile lily. On this day, she began waking up to an uncontrollable coughing fit. Miranda went to get the doctor, but I did not have a good feeling.

The doctor saw her and came out into the hall where I was pacing. He said, "Annabel, she is asking for you. She doesn't have much time. I know she wants to say some things to you, but please do not let her struggle too much."

"Yes, Doctor, I understand."

I walked into Aunt Sarah's room with trepidation. She was so puny, and I was so scared. From my parents' tender love to hers, she has nurtured me into who I am now. Seeing her like this made my heart break. "Auntie, I just spoke with the doctor. He said you were asking for me."

"Yes, Annabel, I was," she paused to take a deeper breath to continue, "I am so proud of the woman you have become. For quite a while, I was worried about you. After that Parker business, I nearly thought I had lost you to your own misery. I realized that time would heal all wounds, and it did. Once I'm gone, time will also heal those wounds."

I tried to say something, but she stopped me. "Please don't interrupt me dear. I haven't much time left. Edgar is waiting for me. I can see him now faintly. He keeps reaching his hand out to me, but I keep telling him, not yet. Here is what I am telling you now, please listen and always remember this. Don't stew in your misery over me. I had a wonderful life and these last few years with you gave me fervor for life like you wouldn't have known. I know you will grieve; you must. That is what makes us human. Also, do not give up on love. There is some young man who has been waiting for you to come along. He will appear as if sent to you by fate. Trust your gut. I think if you had followed the signs with Parker, you would have told him goodbye long before he proposed. He was not right for you. You had nothing in common, but you were enamored because he was your first love. I know I and the Richardson's pushed you together. For that I apologize. I realized too late, he was rotten. People need to say what they mean instead of holding it all in because of pleasantries." She said as she began to cough again.

"Aunt Sarah, please don't work yourself up." I returned as I grabbed her hand.

"Dear child, promise me you will be strong. Sell my house; you don't need it. Move to your house by the sea and enjoy your life. Painting, travel, make friends. Please promise me now." She pleaded.

"I promise Auntie. I promise!" I exclaimed as tears were rolling down my cheeks.

"I see Edgar now coming to take me home. Goodbye my beautiful bright-eyed Annabel. I love you. Don't forget the ro…" Aunt Sarah said as she squeezed my hand one last time and passed away. I sat there for a moment crying, but I knew if she were here with me she would look at me right now and say, "Stop it child. You have many things to take care of now without me." So, I took a deep breath and wiped my tears.

"Goodbye Auntie. Rest in peace now with Edgar." I said as I kissed her hand and gently folded it over her bosom. I walked out of the room to let the doctor know.

The attorney helped me make the arrangements for her funeral. I had her buried next to Edgar as I knew that is what she wanted. The day of the funeral was a sunlit day with few clouds where many of the people she knew came to pay her respects. I placed one of her black, red roses on her grave. They were so magnificent: the darkness balanced with the raw beauty. I rode home in the carriage to find Mrs. Prosper had beaten me home. She wanted to speak to me. "Miss Annabel, I know how hard it is going to be without Miss Clemmons for you and me. I was with her for so long, I don't know how to do anything else."

"Mrs. Prosper, my aunt wanted me to take care of you after she was gone. She had the attorney arrange for you to move to a little cottage not far from here. If you go by her attorney's office tomorrow, he can talk with you about all the details. She left you a sum to also help you along where you can retire. She said you took better care of her than her own mother and she wanted to gift this to you as a way of saying thank you." I explained.

"What a dear lady she was. I loved her so. Thank you, Miss Annabel. I am so happy Miranda will be living with you soon. I hope you two share the same type of bond your auntie and I shared." She said as we hugged one another for a long time, crying, yet knowing, we were going to be okay.

Over the next few days, Miranda and I worked with a group the attorney sent to move some of the furniture and our personal things to my new, old home. Mrs. Prosper settled into her new little cottage quite comfortably. The attorney took care of placing Auntie's house for sale. Mrs. Madalena also stopped by before I made the final move to check on me, seeing that I was doing delightfully well considering all the circumstances.

On the day I was in Aunt Sarah's house for the last time, I walked through every room reliving memories of days gone by since I was fifteen when I moved in with her. Those were bittersweet times as I realized I have come full circle of arriving as a child to leaving as a lady, still in bittersweet times. Oh, how life does play those tricks on us. I shut the back door and walked into the garden. I hoped whoever moved into the house would take care of all the grandeur it held. As I was about to go through the garden gate, I went over and picked one budding black, red rose from the rosebush that bore it. I held it to my nose and all I could smell was the memory of Aunt Sarah. I walked around to my carriage and never looked back.

Chapter 24

I decided to take several months off from painting to just reflect on the past and where my future was moving. Miranda was doing a superb job of taking care of the house and she was truly becoming my companion. I don't think I could live in this house alone.

Those first few months flew by as spring blossomed with daffodils dancing their way into the world once again. Then, summer arrived with warmth and tranquility wafting off the ocean breeze where I could contemplate my life. During this time, I healed from all the pain I have endured from the losses in my life. It was time to be joyous again.

I began painting in late summer, painting the beach, the ocean, from sea to sky. It was breathtaking. One day as I was about to walk near the cliff's edge, I gathered my parents' garden from the corner of my eye. I sauntered over to it and looked in. I felt ashamed. I was so consumed in my own selfish world, I forgot to check on it. At this point, I didn't think I had the energy to restart it. This made me go back into the house restructuring my day. I changed my plans. I knew what I should be doing with my time.

I decided to walk into town because the day was shining down on me as the sun guided me like a guardian angel. My destination was the gallery to talk with Mr. Christopher. I went into the gallery and found him sitting at his desk working on some paperwork. "Good day, Mr. Christopher."

He looked up as if I startled him because he was engrossed in his work. "Miss Allan, it is so nice to see you again. My condolences to your aunt's departure. She was truly a lovely lady."

"Thank you, I appreciate your sentiments." I added as I looked down trying not to focus on Aunt Sarah's passing.

"So, what brings you by today?" He asked.

"Well, I've moved to the house my parents owned when I was a child. I am settled in, and I need something to satisfy my time. I know I stopped doing commissions a while ago, but I think I want to begin anew. I have been painting, and I know I can get right back into it without hesitation."

Mr. Christopher smiled happily, "That would be splendid. I don't know how quickly we can get you started; however, I have people coming in every day. So, I might have work for you before too long."

"Thank you, Mr. Christopher. You don't know how much this means to me." I shook his hand, and he offered to show me around the gallery to view some of the new paintings he added since I was here last before I started back home feeling elated at the news of completing portraits.

Within a month, Mr. Christopher had an abundance of work for me. Fall began to appear with just the hint of some color in the leaves of the oak and maple trees throughout town.

With the cooler temperatures moving down the thermometer, it allowed me to really focus on my work. For me to do this, I took the room off the kitchen, which had large windows facing the garden, and turned it into my art studio. I could see the ocean and all of nature's glory surrounding the area. It brought me peace and opened my mind to creativity.

Chapter 25

Living by the ocean offered me the best muse for creating my art. The sound of the waves each morning set my emotions in tune with my soul emitting through my fingertips with electricity pulsing through the brush to my canvas. My ocean view was rapturous since my home was built on a cliff looking down to the water's edge crashing into the modicum of rocks used as nature's drum with the water beating musically every day and night. Housing my art studio at home, I rarely left except to walk to the village nearby for my wares. Miranda kept herself busy all the time doing this or that around the house. However, she was always scheduled to attend to me on days I was meeting with potential clients, or I was painting a man's portrait.

It was a calm, brisk wintry morning, as I waited for my client's son, my latest commission, my latest subject to paint, on this first day of December in the year 1849. At a previous gallery event, the man's father admired my work. Mr. Christopher visited me the previous week to set up all the details. The client's name was Mr. Wilson. Mr. Christopher told me he asked me to paint his son's portrait as a gift to his wife. As I prepared my supplies and tools, I heard two polite knocks at my front door.

"Miranda, would you please answer the door?" I asked, patting my hair and straightening my dress in the mirror in my sitting room. I heard footsteps entering lightly as I turned around to find Miranda with a young man in uniform. Mr. Wilson failed to mention his son was affiliated with the military; therefore, this realization caused me to mildly palpitate due to his handsome demeanor as he peered into my very soul with his radiant chestnut eyes. "Mr. Wilson, I presume? Your father said you would arrive efficiently on time."

"It is Lieutenant Arthur Wilson, ma'am. Pleased to make your acquaintance." Responding as he reached for my hand to softly shake it, never moving his eyes away from mine.

"Thank you, so pleasant to meet you. I am Annabel Allan. This is my lady's maid, Miss Miranda Rodgers. Shall we have a seat and discuss the portrait before we begin the sitting?" I asked as I moved my hand toward a chair for him to sit. We began discussing the elements he would like me to highlight in the portrait. I tried to focus on our conversation, but I have never felt this way about meeting anyone for the first time. This man was so handsome with thick wavy black hair, his compassionate soulful dark eyes, his stoic mustache, and his eloquent southern accent.

"Miss Allan, does that satisfy the information you need for the portrait?" he quizzically asked.

Still slightly dazed, "Oh, yes, yes, that will be fine." Blushing as pink as a pig, I responded, stood up, and suggested, "Shall we move into my studio to begin."

We walked down the hallway into the studio, a large room with half walls where the windows widely showed the outdoors surrounding the house. I had the lieutenant sit down on a high back chair. It was the high-back chair I brought from Aunt Sarah's house. I hope he felt as comfortable as I do when I sit in it. As I did my sketch work, he remained quiet, allowing me to concentrate, but I could feel him studying me. Or was he just watching my process?

After an hour and a half, I had what I needed for my sketches. "Lieutenant, we are finished with your first session. I..."

Suddenly, Miranda interrupted, "Ma'am, I have lunch. And, uh, plenty for a guest if you know what I mean."

The lieutenant looked away with a half-smile at Miranda's obvious hint for him to stay. "Well, uh, Lieutenant, do you have plans for lunch? According to Miranda, we may accommodate a guest."

He replied, "Unfortunately, I do have other engagements to attend, but thank you Miss Allan and Miss Rodgers." He put on his coat, and I walked him to the door. "When should I return for my next session?"

"If you could come back tomorrow, it would be quite helpful. Your father wants to give this to your mother for Christmas. It is possible, but I must work each day."

"Then I will be back at the same time tomorrow morning. Until then." he said as he put his hat on and walked out the door to his coach to leave.

"I would be smitten with him if I didn't have my beau." Miranda giggled.

"Oh Miranda, he is a handsome man!" I paused, "Until tomorrow..."

Chapter 26

The next day arrived when he was punctual again. We started immediately, and the time went as fast as a cat chasing a mouse. Earlier that morning, I told Miranda to hold lunch until he had left. I did not want to make him feel uncomfortable by asking him to stay again where he might not be able to. I finished and expected him to leave, but he moved into my sitting room with me, and we talked for thirty more minutes. I learned a little about his family and some of his sea voyages, which were fascinating. I did not want him to leave, but he looked at his pocket watch and realized he was late for an appointment. We said our adieus and he promised to return the next day.

He did return the next day, and the next, and all the days following. Each day he stayed a little longer with the eighth day staying for lunch. Miranda served lunch in the studio where I had a small, intimate table and chairs. I liked to eat there from time to time to enjoy the scenery. I knew he would enjoy the view. "Miss Allan, may I call you Annabel?" he hesitantly asked.

"Why yes. I would be honored."

"I noticed the other day you have what looks to be a divine garden area behind your studio."

I replied, "Yes, there is a garden. My parents gardened when I was a child. After they departed, I did not have the heart to keep it going once I moved back to this house earlier this year."

"I am so sorry for your loss. If you don't mind me asking, how old were you when they died?"

"I was fifteen and I was staying with my aunt. My father was travelling for his business, and my mother went with him. They were staying in a hotel, there was a fire, and they were trapped. I remained with my aunt until she died. Once I turned twenty-one, I received a trust. I decided to move here and began taking art commissions." I explained.

"That must have been difficult being so young. You have made a charming home here though. It is so quaint and beautiful," he responded.

"Why, thank you. Before my aunt died, she helped me redecorate and I could not be happier."

"I also noticed the flowers you keep in your parlor and your studio. The scent is quite nice. You have an eye for them. I guess that is one of the reasons you do such striking art. The roses…are they your favorite?"

"Why yes. When I go into town, I like to go by the flower market and pick some. The blue-red roses were my mother's favorite, the black-red roses were my aunt's favorite, and I have been choosing this deep dark red rose with a touch of ivory as my favorite. It is so quaint you noticed them. Do you like gardening?"

He returned, "Actually, I do. To me, flowers in a woman's home are just a metaphor for her beauty. The black-red rose compliments the darkness of your hair, the blue-red rose compliments the brightness of your eyes, and the ivory-red rose compliments your alabaster skin. It is a trifecta of pure exquisiteness," he paused and continued, "Um, Miss Annabel, I would like to request the honor of your company tomorrow evening. My parents are having a dinner party, and I would like you to be my guest. I will pick you up at six."

"I accept." And with this acceptance, my entire world changed. Arthur returned each day so I could finish the portrait. He returned with loving eyes and a cherished heart for me. He brought me a deep velvety red rose with a hint of cream at the center each day.

"Arthur, you are spoiling me with these magnificent roses."

"You deserve to be given flowers every time I see you. I chose this rose to bring because you said it was the one you decided was your favorite. The black-red and the blue-red belonged to important ladies in your life. Those were their choices. This one is yours. I found out this red and ivory rose is called Dark Night."

"How enchanting! It sounds so romantic and mysterious."

"Yes, the romanticism in this rose brings out your joy and energy. There is no question, and there is no mystery, the *angels from Heaven above* guided me to your door." Arthur gently said giving me chills at his romantic nature for such a seemingly strong man.

One night after he left, I was holding the rose he brought that day and smelling the heavenly scent wafting from the gentle petals. A memory of Aunt Sarah came to mind. It was the tragic story of her time with her beau. She told me he had brought her deep black-red roses. She also told me to choose a rose to be mine! How I had forgotten, but without cognizance, I did choose my rose, a Dark Night. This seemed so bittersweet, but at the same time, it brought me closer to Aunt Sarah. She basically said to not squander time when it came to love. Smelling the rose again, I said aloud, "This is love. I do love Arthur!"

Chapter 27

A few days before Christmas, I finished the painting, which I think I painted my love into his face. I started wondering when he might be leaving again for his next voyage, but I was afraid to ask, but I knew I must. "Arthur, when do you go back out to sea?" I cut right to it.

He walked over to me, placing his hands at the small of my back while I shivered from his warmth. "I leave on January 1st. I should have told you sooner, but I didn't want to face the day either."

"I see, that is soon, but it is not like I will never see you again."

"My darling, my beautiful Annabel, you are so right. It will be a short journey, then I will be back." Saying reassuringly.

He knew Miranda was not far away and was probably listening and even watching us, as all good lady's maids do, but he threw caution to the wind. Bending down, he cupped my cheek with his hand and kissed me for the first time. At that moment, I wholeheartedly knew our souls would *never dissever*.

Chapter 28

Christmas day arrived. I had a new dark green dress made for the occasion. Arthur picked me up to spend time with his family and deliver the painting. We arrived promptly. His mother was so surprised with the painting; she loved it. We dined together and enjoyed company by the fire as it was quite a chilly day. Arthur asked me to accompany him to the library.

"Arthur, I have had the most wonderful time with you and your family. I feel so at home with you." I glowed.

"Well, I am very happy to hear that because I want to ask you something." He hinted.

"Oh, what? Plans for tomorrow?"

"Um, not necessarily plans for tomorrow."

"I'm sorry, I should not have assumed…" I felt embarrassed.

Arthur interrupted, "Plans forever. Will you marry me?" He asked as he bent down on one knee holding a decadent opal ring. "I have loved you from the moment I saw you."

"Arthur, my dearest, I love you too and I will marry you!" I exclaimed.

At that, he placed the ring on my finger, stood up, folded me into his arms and kissed me again with more passion than I thought possible. "Annabel, let's go tell my parents. Since I am scheduled to leave January 1st, let's marry tomorrow. I know this seems so fast, but I can't fathom one more day of being apart from you. What do you say?"

Answering with utter delight, "Yes, I love it!"
As we told his parents, they were ecstatic, welcoming me to the family, hugging and fussing all over me. His mother took me aside and said I could wear her wedding gown, and she would have the minister come to the house tomorrow afternoon.

Chapter 29

We were married the next day; everything was pure bliss. It was enchanting outside because it had started to snow Christmas night. Arthur made sure I had a bouquet of the Dark Night roses to hold for the ceremony.

On this day, I was not nervous at all. I knew this is where I was supposed to be, and I knew Arthur was the man I was supposed to be with. Once Aunt Sarah said there was a man waiting for me, and she was right. I didn't feel this when I was with Parker. He wasn't interested in anything I did or said, but Arthur was interested in me and I in him. This month had been a whirlwind of emotions only to end with a lifetime of forevers.

When Mrs. Wilson came to get me, she looked me over and said, "Annabel, you are gorgeous both inside and out. You are the most lovely bride I have ever seen. You wear your love for Arthur as a badge of loveliness for my son. I am so proud today I may call you daughter."

I almost started to cry, but I held back and grinned loudly. I stood looking in the mirror at myself in awe of the incredibly dainty ivory gown she had let me wear. The dress was off the shoulders, but had a lace yoke scrolling up to the neck with pearl buttons flowing down the front. The silk seemed to glow as it was sleek as the oil lamps shined on distinct parts of the dress. My dark hair was placed up at the back of my neck as it was the color of coffee contrasting with the pureness of the ivory of the fabric. My bouquet matched perfectly as the creamy centers stood out to cradle the dark red. I was ready to be Arthur's bride forevermore.

As I walked through the doorway to the parlor, the minister and Arthur were standing by the fireplace. Mrs. Wilson lit some candles. With that light in addition to the light from the fireplace, the ambiance of the room seemed magical. Arthur and I locked eyes with each other as I walked toward him. I wasn't just walking toward the man I loved; I was walking to my forever future. He took my hand, leaned down to me, and whispered, "You are the most breathtaking being I have ever seen." As he stood upright, he just grazed my cheek with his tender lips. My knees weakened just enough for me to feel the shivers of his passion from that one tiny gesture. The minister went through the ceremony and had us recite our vows.

"Arthur, I take you as my husband to obey, cherish, and love with every waking day, every moment of bliss and heartache until the end of time, until we are parted by death. I love you with every fiber of my being and every ounce of my soul. I will honor you all the days we spend together and all the days we are separated by your voyages at sea. Arthur, you are my one and only love, forevermore."

"Annabel, I take you as my wife to love, honor, and cherish you every day until the end of time. You are the star who guides me at sea and the compass that carries me back to you. I have longed for the love we share. With this love, I will be true to you forevermore. I will take care of you for the rest of your life. You will want for nothing, and my love is infinite and will stand the test of time. My beloved Annabel, you represent the poetry my heart sings. I am your protector, your light, and your love until time stops as we are intertwined as one."

The minister pronounced us as Mr. and Mrs. Arthur W. Wilson. His parents hugged us both. The minister hugged me and shook Arthur's hand. I didn't want this day to end. I wish my parents and Aunt Sarah would have been here with me, but I knew they were here in spirit. I felt the vibrance of their love all around me as if they were hugging me through the spectral plane. After all the pleasantries, we went into the dining room to celebrate.

Chapter 30

After a splendid wedding feast with his parents, we went back to my home by carriage ride. I smiled because it was now our home. I felt as if we were in a fairy tale with snow covered grounds that were untouched by footsteps this grand evening. As we approached the drive, Arthur held me tight kissing my cheek, nuzzling me just so where his mustache tickled me with delight.

Exiting the carriage on the last step down, I pulled up my dress so I would not get it in the snow, but Arthur realized it was unavoidable. "Darling, allow me," as he swept me up in his arms and carried me over the threshold of our home into the entrance way. The gesture was so romantic, I was overcome with emotion almost dizzy; however, only the dizziness of being loved so fully. Everything Arthur did made me love him even more so. He pulled me in close and kissed me zealously, building a fire within me. He paused and seemed excited about something.

"My darling, I have a surprise for you." Arthur whispered with glee. "Tomorrow afternoon, we are to leave by train to travel to New York City for a short honeymoon for a few days."

I squealed, "Oh Arthur, how wonderful!"

We made plans to pack the next morning and discussed what we would like to do in the city. The fire was starting to burn down, filling the room with a slight chill. "You go prepare for bed and I will go out and get more firewood." Arthur suggested.

I went to my room with a feeling of warmth and love, thinking how did I find such a wonderful man, but then I started thinking of how soon he had to go away. I brushed it off, staying positive, because I would treasure every moment we were together; alternatively, upon his absences to the sea, I would yearn for him to return, which would feel as if we were meeting for the first time repeatedly.

Brushing my hair, I realized Arthur should have already returned inside. I went to the window in my sitting room to look out, but I did not see him. I put on my coat to check outside. Opening the door, I saw him laying down on the ground, wood everywhere. I ran to him. "Arthur, what happened?"

Grunting with pain, "I think I broke my leg!"

Hurriedly, I ran to one of the neighbors for help. The man and his son were able to help Arthur back indoors. The man's other son went to get the town doctor. Arthur had indeed broken his leg. "Darling Annabel, I am so sorry we must change our plans. I wholeheartedly wanted to show you New York. We must cancel our trip."

"Arthur, my dearest, this cannot be helped. I will nurture you back to health. I love you with all my heart and soul." I beamed as I bent down to kiss him.

"I *love you with a love that is more than love* forevermore!" He responded with another kiss and a warm embrace, "Annabel, in the morning, would you mind going into town with a letter to my commanding officer about my situation?"

"Of course."

The next morning, I went into town and provided a letter to Arthur's commanding officer about his leg. He was very obliging and polite with wedding congratulations when he handed me a letter to return to Arthur.

Upon arriving home, Arthur immediately read the letter with a grand smile on his face. "My bright-eyed beauty, Captain Guy granted me four months leave!" We hugged and fervidly kissed, knowing we were stealing time before he had to return to the sea. The broken leg was unfortunate, but the broken leg gave us a deeper connection to each other.

Chapter 31

Over the next few months, we grew closer together each day. We were so close that anyone would *covet our love* if they saw us together, even *the demons down under the sea*. While he was still bedridden, I would read to him poetry and stories that became our favorites, not to pass the time, but to enhance our relationship by finding out our likes and dislikes. I found we both loved Edgar Allan Poe's poems, so I frequently loved reading these aloud, but so did Arthur. As he read Poe's second version of *To Helen*, he paused after a moment:

Clad all in white, upon a violet bank
I saw thee half reclining; while the moon
Fell on the upturn'd faces of the roses,
And on thine own, upturn'd — alas! in sorrow!

"Annabel, I think of you on our wedding day when I read this, except you were not in sorrow, you were encapsulated by love. This is such a romantic poem, a gesture of love by Poe. I am so enamored by your sweetness, your beauty, and your love. This time together solidifies everything I already knew about you. I love reading together. I can't wait until I am out of this bed so we can experience the sunlight walking along the shore."

"Arthur, I feel the same way. It will be just a little more time and then we can. Patience, my love." At that, Arthur finished the poem and then pulled me onto the bed with him rapturously showing how much he loved me.

Chapter 32

Once Arthur could walk with a cane, the weather started becoming more pleasant, so we would sit together and watch the ocean roar singing our favorite tune. By the end of March, Arthur suggested we renovate the garden area and create a rose garden.

"Annabel, how would you feel about clearing out the garden area? We could start from scratch with something new."

I thought about it for a moment before answering. I thought how my parents thrived in that very garden, and it seemed like it didn't just grow flowers and plants, but it grew their love for each other. "Arthur, I think that is a splendid idea. My parents would be so proud to know we reenergized the garden that brought them so much pleasure."

"What type of garden did they have?" He asked.

"They planted all kinds of flowers and plants. It was quite lovely."

Arthur thought for a moment as he squinted his brows making his whole face look crooked, but rather cute in a way crinkling his mustache. "How about a rose garden?"

"Yes, I think that would be so charming! I love the idea! Thank you my dear."

"We'll begin tomorrow clearing it out. That will give us plenty of time to decide how many rose bushes we need, or want, and which kind."

It took us several weeks working through pulling weeds, digging up old dead bushes, and tilling up the soil so it would be fresh and ready when we began to plant the rose bushes. One pleasant day, we rode in our carriage into town to choose our roses. On the way we discussed things we thought we wanted. "Annabel, upon measuring, I think we can fit around a dozen rose bushes where they will not be crowded, and the square space will feel exactly right. Thoughts?"

"I like that idea; it would be very balanced. Could we get different varieties of roses?"

"Of course, darling. I love the idea of a mixture of colors. However, I must insist we find at least one Dark Night rose bush." Arthur added adamantly.

"Absolutely," I said as I kissed him. We arrived and began to look through multiple types of rose bushes.

Together we chose twelve rose bushes of varying colors of reds, pinks, yellows, and whites. We were quite saddened when we found out the proprietor did not have any Dark Night rose bushes. I kept this to myself, but I hoped this was not some kind of omen. I had to tell my brain not to worry and shutter that feeling away. Once we were finished, we headed home and enjoyed a perfectly calm evening together watching the sunset as we knew the rose bushes would be delivered the next day where our work would be hearty.

For the next week, we worked from dawn until dusk each day adding three rose bushes near each wall. We also added a walking path so we could peruse the garden with steady feet. We used stones from around the property as step stones. At the end of the week, we eyed the garden in great splendor. The hard work paid off and we were left with a beautiful sight to enjoy our time together before Arthur had to leave. I knew the time was drawing near as my conscience kept hinting at me like a devil on my shoulder.

Chapter 33

For the next month, we walked through the garden each morning and each night admiring our handy work. Arthur was fully healed. We knew the inevitable was coming–Arthur would be leaving May 1st. The month of April was filled with bittersweet moments of bliss. We spent every moment together. We read to each other, we walked together, and we made love intensely every day filling our rapturous souls to the brim savoring our love in the absence of Arthur as we would be parted for a short while. Our souls were one. I could not fathom being without him, but *our love was stronger by far than the love of those older than we*.

April 30th arrived; I had a sinking feeling in my stomach knowing this was our last day together. When I went into the kitchen, Arthur was nowhere around. He had allowed me to sleep in, so it was closer to ten o'clock. I saw no remnants of breakfast and asked Miranda where Arthur was. "Ma'am, he left earlier this morning, but he has been out in the garden for about an hour."

I walked outside to find Arthur bent down in the center of the garden looking a little disheveled. "Good morning, Dearest. What are you doing, pray tell?"

"Good morning, Darling. Once we finished our garden, I always felt as if it needed one more rose bush. I went into town early and picked this up." He said pointing to a Dark Night rose bush placed directly in the center of the garden.

"It is perfect as our love." We kissed as he drew me into him. "I was so sad when we didn't find that variety when we planted the garden. I can't believe you found one today."

"The proprietor just had this one as if it were waiting for us to bring it home. I thought the perfect place was right here in the center as if the other twelve rose bushes were blanketing our love." Arthur poetically answered.

Our last day together was one of the most romantic days we spent. We picnicked on the beach with a lovely lunch prepared by Miranda, we read to each other, and we walked in our rose garden nuzzling, kissing passionately and progressively. We went back into the house that night giving in again to the desire we had for each other.

Chapter 34

The next morning arrived with vengeance, but I knew he had to go to his other lady–the sea. He walked me to our rose garden for our adieus. "My darling Annabel, I will only be gone for a few months and then I will return to our *kingdom by the sea*. Promise me you will look after our rose garden as if it is my very love that binds us. My love for you is stronger than anything or anyone. On nights you long to be with me, look at the Dark Night rose bush and know I am out there dreaming of you. The rose bush is our sign I will return to you always."

"Arthur, I love you more than you know. *I have no other thoughts than to love you*. I promise these roses will last the test of time to grow our love forevermore." I returned weeping as we cradled each other in our arms for several minutes. He wiped my tears away and kissed me as if it were our last.

Chapter 35

Two months passed leaving me sullen every day, but trying to look forward to Arthur's homecoming. Miranda brought me the mail. In the stack was a letter officially marked by the Navy. Opening rapidly, the words leapt off the page like daggers to my heart–Arthur was lost at sea. I screamed and fainted, letting the letter fall to the floor.

Arthur's parents collected me and brought me to stay with them. Miranda attended my house and visited me when she could. I withdrew from everyone for the next few months grieving for my husband. How could this be? They must find him. No one could console the utter grief driving through my mortally wounded soul.

Chapter 36

"Arthur, Arthur! Where are you?" I would dream I was on a ship looking for you in the water, looking for you in other lands, but finding nothing. Then I would dream about the months we shared together in our newlywed days of utter bliss and ignorance, unknowingly blind to what would happen to you. The dreams were strong every night for days, weeks, and months. You were there as if you had not left, and then it seemed as if you were dead and gone from this world. Fortunately, my dreams were reminiscent of the best times we shared.

Months turned into years as I finally moved back to the cottage after a year with no word on Arthur. Finally, one morning, I walked into the garden finding it in disarray. Wait, I promised him I would cultivate it like our love. For the next few months, I brought it back to life, except for one rose bush, the yellow one died. My soul kept tearing away.

Even with precise pruning and care, one rose bush died every year. As each one gave up its life with no news of Arthur, a little part of me died, leaving me with a heart condition.

Chapter 37

Twelve years passed, still not giving up hope, I became terribly ill with Miranda and Arthur's parents at my bedside each day. They set up a bed in my studio so I could look out at the Dark Night rose bush, the embodiment of mine and Arthur's love. The only rose bush hanging on.

On May 1st, twelve years to the day Arthur left my side, I felt the urge to go outside, to feel the sea air against my skin, to walk in the rose garden, and to smell the sweet scent of the last evidence of our love.

Miranda was out doing her shopping, and the Wilsons were at home, so no one would stop me. I crept out of my bed walking slowly to the Dark Night. I did not know what I would find, but those roses were calling me like a siren. As I was before the rose bush, I bent gently down and smelled it, my hand fell on it grasping one of the roses as it broke off in my feeble hand as I collapsed to the ground.

Chapter 38

The air was alive with a dark aroma spinning through the salty sea air as it whipped across the rose garden. Unbalanced steps on the path to the garden could be heard as a cane created an echo of quickness to arrive promptly. As he approached the Dark Night, he saw a lifeless body laying before it. He grabbed her up, embracing her to find her faintly breathing. "My darling, my darling, Annabel, I am here! I am so sorry!"

He held her like they were one, wailing with tears streaming like raindrops. He looked upon her face hoping he was not too late.

A stir was felt from his frail love. "Arthur, I never gave up hope." She whispered as she clung to every breath.

"My ship had an accident. I was hurt, almost left for dead. I was rescued, but I could not remember any of my life, except I knew someone was bringing me dreams of home every time I smelled or saw a Dark Night rose or rose bush. Two weeks ago, my memory came back. I rushed as fast as I could. I am here now and my love for you is stronger than ever before. I will never leave you!"

Arthur picked up Annabel. Walking the path away from the rose bush that solidified their love so long ago, the rose bush would live on for their children, and multitudes of children over time infinitely, forevermore.

Epilogue

Arthur and Annabel lived in their *kingdom by the sea* for the rest of their lives. He resigned from the Navy and joined his father in the family business so he would never be apart from Annabel again.

Annabel grew stronger and continued to paint and take on commissions at the house building a repertoire of her work for many families to cherish for several generations. She and Arthur planted more rose bushes in the garden so the Dark Night would not be alone. In addition to the rose bush having companions, they welcomed a son, Arthur, Jr. the following year. Within two years, they had a daughter named after her mother and her aunt, Sarah Adalaide.

They raised their family joyfully creating happy moments and memories their children would treasure. Arthur Jr. and Sarah grew up to be sweet mannered young people finding their own loves, getting married, and having children of their own.

Arthur and Annabel lived on into their eighties, never leaving their home situated by the *sounding sea*. To celebrate their 60th wedding anniversary, their children came to visit for the Christmas holidays in December 1909. They had a marvelous dinner together. Arthur and Annabel could not have been more happy than seeing how their children and grandchildren had prospered.

The next morning, Arthur, Jr. went to wake them up for breakfast, but was surprised his father had not risen earlier than he always did. He went to knock on the door to their room, but did not hear a sound. He peeked in and saw them lying together in each other's arms. He could tell, their *high-born kinsmen came and bore them away* from him and his sister. He was sad, but he knew they were together forevermore.

Arthur Jr. had them buried under their Dark Night rose bush together in the same coffin. He knew they should not be separated, even at death. On the headstone was inscribed the following:

Entwined in love

Interred as one

Memorialized forevermore

Arthur William Wilson

&

Annabel Lee Wilson

And so, all the night-tide, I lie down by the side

Of my darling — my darling — my life and my bride,

In our sepulchre there by the sea —

In our tomb by the sounding sea.

The End.

Acknowledgements

This book would not be possible without the sheer genius of Edgar Allan Poe. I have loved the poem, Annabel Lee, since the first time I heard it many and many years ago. It is so beautiful, and bittersweet all rolled up into this poetical tune. A few years ago, I thought about writing Annabel Lee's story, but it was not sitting in my brain in just the right chair. A few months ago, I entered a short story contest where they choose the genre and a few other details. The story must be completed within a week. I have done these challenges before, and I always hope for mystery, horror, thriller, but this time I was assigned romance. So, the origins of *The Rose Bush* are embedded in two ideas. The first is from a trip my husband and I were on during Thanksgiving in 2024. We were in North Carolina and did a train ride. Looking out the window, I saw a large backyard with one rose bush in the very center of the yard. I took a picture and in my Google Keep, my digital brain, storing all my ideas, I recorded the note of one rose bush in a backyard, knowing I would use it for either a story or poem. The second is in my short story, Annabel Lee's back story; however, I did give her a different ending. I hope Mr. Poe agrees with me.

One of my very great friends who told me this would make a nice novella was Holly Knightley. At first, I was skeptical because romance? I normally do not write in that style, but she encouraged me to try it. Once I figured out where to begin, it was like Annabel Lee took over my keyboard and poured her heart out on the digital pages. Thank you Holly so much! I could not have done this without your positive words of inspiration.

I also want to thank my dear friend and POEcast partner in crime, Jeanie Smith. She read the short story, gave me feedback, and then read the novella, and gave me feedback. She is critical, but with a constructive pen. Everything we do with our podcast supports Mr. Poe and how he has influenced so many things in the world. We have the best time planning episodes and ideas. I could not do this podcast with anyone else! Thank you Jeanie for inspiring me with your creativity and knowledge.

In school, I had two teachers who highly motivated me to write. I shared my stories with them, and they gave me feedback. My fourth-grade teacher, Mrs. Sandra Deripaska, at the time allowed me to share a story with the class leaving it open ended. All my classmates had to write an ending to this murder mystery, and I chose the best one. The other teacher who encouraged me was my eleventh and twelfth grade English teacher, Mrs. Jo Davis, God rest her soul. She read a murder mystery I wrote in the seventh grade and told me what I needed to do to make it top notch. I have been working on that periodically ever since. I hope to one day publish it.

I also want to say a heavenly thank you to my parents who both passed many years ago. They both encouraged me to be all I could be. I was a weird kid, and I know I am a weird adult, and I owe them so much for allowing me to love murder mysteries, be picky, and be the odd one out. I love them for that!

I wholeheartedly want to thank my husband, Jeff, for everything he is and does. Without him, also allowing me to be my weird self, I could not do what I do. Any time I want to go to another state to find Poe connections, he is right there creating an itinerary and leading the way. He encourages my creativity whether it be writing, sewing, or art. He listens to my poems and short stories at length and provides plot hole feedback. He never complains and pushes me to go for what I want in my career and my hobbies. I have never had this kind of support before. Forevermore, I love you, Jeff!

About the Author

Carmen Bouldin works as an English teacher. She has worked in education since 2004. In her spare time, she writes gothic romance, mystery, and poetry. Much of her writing and art is inspired by Edgar Allan Poe. Her poem, "The Raven's Mourning," was nominated for a Saturday Visiter Award in 2020. This poem was also published in Raven's Quoth Press' poetry anthology, *Evermore*, in 2024. She also cohosts a podcast, The Six Degrees of Edgar A. Poe, where she and her POEcast partner, Jeanie Smith, discuss Poe's influences on multiple genres. She also enjoys creating visual art. Her painting, "There's no Place like Poe," was nominated for a Saturday Visiter Award in 2019. A native Memphian, Carmen, resides in Middle Tennessee with her husband, Jeff, and their two cats, tuxedo cat-Mitt and solid black cat-Poe. Carmen and Jeff love to travel and wear vintage inspired attire Carmen creates through the art of sewing.

You may find Carmen's writing, art, and sewing at the following:

Website: https://thequotableraven.com/

Facebook - @thequotableraven

X - @thequoteraven

Instagram - @ravenmade23

You may find Carmen and Jeanie's POEcast at:

www.sixdegreesofpoe.com

Facebook – @the6degreesofedgarallanpoe

X – @sixdegreesofpoe

Instagram – @sixdegreesofpoe

Spotify –
https://open.spotify.com/show/09UNSDV4ZXIEf19ZhQwJ63?si=49
fa62b4329441ba

YouTube - https://www.youtube.com/@poeunplugged3978